Beast

of the

Night

E.E. Rawls

Titles by E.E. Rawls

Earthaverse:

Draev Guardians Series

Strayborn (1)

Dragons & Ravens (1.5)

Strayblood (2)

Alteredverse:

Frost, Winter's Lonely Guardian

Portal to Eartha

Beast of the Night

Madness Solver in Wonderland

Coming Soon:

Straypath (3)

Secret projects ;)

Find out when the next books are releasing, and get exclusive content, by following my newsletter at:
eerawls.com

Love is patient, love is kind.
A tale as old as time…

ROSENROT TRIED TO WARM HER chilled fingers with her breath. Heavy clouds made the day feel later than it actually was, rolling gray and depressing overhead. The leaves crunched under her careful footsteps, and twigs rustled and clawed at her frock coat. A sea of red surrounded her—trees and brush red as blood with autumn—as she navigated the path that had once been a road, now an overgrown trail through the forest.

Hidden above the valley, in the foothills of the mountains, some said there was an ancient castle, whose masters had once ruled over the town snug in the valley below.

Rosen was new to Freudendorf Town. Her drunk of a father had moved him and her motherless self here to this quaint, tucked away place of half-timbered buildings (which reminded her of gingerbread houses) and cobblestone streets. He was hiding from the debt collectors, and what better way to do it than in a town few knew of?

Dad said the world had changed a lot since World War III, and the following Solar Storm Wipeout. He used that as an excuse for his behavior and lack of desire to earn an honest wage, claiming that the world owed him for his past childhood hardships.

Rosen tried not to feel lonely and bored, having no friends to talk to, but busied herself with exploring the new town environment and reading old books. Freudendorf kids eyed her with suspicion like a newcomer invading their peaceful lives whenever she walked by.

The surrounding foothills and sharp mountains stood like giants ringing the horizon every which way she turned, guarding against the outside world beyond the valley—or keeping them trapped inside.

Donning her old frock coat earlier that morning, she had ventured out, wandering the town's narrow streets. The sun was fading in and out between amassing clouds. Somehow the overcast weather made the autumn leaves stand out more vividly—reds, bright oranges and splotchy yellows glowing with a different light.

While wandering, she stumbled upon a dim library, and there picked up a book which spoke of a castle in the foothills. The cover seemed to indicate it was more a recorded history than a fictional tale, and had chapters on other facts about the town, such as the old salt mines—what used to be the town's main source of commerce, a rare type of salt, long ago.

No one used the mines anymore, since they were located in the western foothills—a forbidden area, according to local gossip.

The book was tattered, clearly something old and forgotten. She'd found it at the far back of the library, where the lamplight barely reached.

When she asked the library owner, he didn't say much about it, only that it was a book from way back when. The castle in the western foothills was an abandoned place now, he told her, except for the rumored *Nachzehrer*—the Beast of the Night.

"Beast of the Night?"

"*Ja*, a beast dwells within that forest. Terrifying creature. No one dares go near it." The librarian leaned down, his glasses reflecting lamplight. "It's forbidden territory, those western mountains where the castle sits. Don't you go near it."

Now, here she was, seeking out that forbidden territory, hiking up the first path she came across veering up and away from the town. It was getting late, and an early moon hid somewhere behind the clouds chasing the sun away.

Rosen drew her frayed coat up closer around her neck as a breeze whistled past. Blood leaves danced and swayed. Between gaps in the sea of red above, she could see the clouds frothing angrily and forming precarious spirals. She'd get caught in the storm soon, if she didn't hurry, but curiosity kept her climbing higher.

The air smelled earthy and sweet of rotting leaves. She wiped her dripping nose; it was getting colder. Minutes seemed to inch by, and her shoes felt heavier going uphill. She tipped her head up to the sky one more time, and a gray needle rose to pierce through the mix of forest and storm.

A castle spire.

Her heart did a backflip in her chest, and her footsteps quickened, the spire bobbing up and down in her vision as she ran.

When a wall of bushes obstructed the path, she slowed and worked her way through, shoving and snapping twigs, ignoring their painful scratch.

Aaaah!

Rosen froze.

The strange cry came from up ahead, an echo rolling past her and weaving through the sentinel tree trunks.

She waited for a moment, then crept forward. The bushes opened a fraction and she peeked through.

Beyond was a clearing: where the path became pavestones riddled with weeds and crawling vines, a wide area before a gate which was too far away to see clearly.

The strange cry came again.

Her pulse jolted. She angled her head through the leaves so that her gaze could rove over the clearing, but didn't let herself move any more than that, in case whatever it was might see her.

She spotted something then. A dark shadow rose from the pavestones like a wraith, with something of a cape billowed around its undefined features.

Two perfect circles glowed, eyes like silver coins, tipped up to the sky.

It cried or howled—she couldn't tell which, a sound that rubbed shivers down her spine. The silvery eyes lowered, and slowly turned her way.

A strangled gasp escaped her throat, and she fell backwards.

Vainly trying to stop her fall and the noise she was making, she landed on her palm and backside. Autumn did not let such movements be quiet. The snapping and crunching of dying leaves and underbrush were as loud as a shot gun.

Something like a growl echoed in place of the strange wail from the clearing beyond the bushes.

Rosen scrambled to get up, turning noisily onto her knees and pushing her body up into a run, all caution thrown aside.

Leaves crunched at her back—the wraith was coming after her!

She ran, jumping fallen branches and thick brambles, clutching her coat tightly to keep from getting caught on twigs, hurrying downhill, down the messy red path.

She didn't slow, didn't stop. Didn't turn to look and see when whatever it was finally gave up the chase. She ran with burning lungs back into town.

Six Years Later

Rosenrot tucked a stray wisp of lavender hair back behind her ear. She liked this new color and cut: an angled bob, high in the back and low brushing her shoulders in the front. Compared to all the long, braided hairstyles going around town, this was more unique and suited her complexion. She added a small braid on the side, though, so as not to be too wildly different.

She shifted the basket looped around her left upper arm, tucking what remained of her elbow up like a hook to keep it from falling. The basket held scant groceries of bread and eggs—all she could afford to buy this week, thanks to her father drinking money away.

They'd been poor to begin with—had been for years—and his bad habits kept drying up every bit she tried to save. It didn't matter how well she hid the cash; he seemed to have a special knack for finding it—a well-developed talent that she wished he would put to good use and go get a job.

Really, was that too much to ask? She huffed.

Her nose breathed in the aroma of fresh baking as she walked through town, morning bakeries at work filling the shelves with breads, pastries and gingerbread. It was the best scent, other than old book pages. She adjusted a book under her other elbow, longing to find a moment to dive into its pages.

"*Guten morgen* to you, fair Rosenrot!"

She almost missed a step.

Rosen turned her head, despite the protests whirling in her stomach. "Oh, *guten morgen*, Duke Gasto," she forced herself to reply.

Her feet continued forward, not wanting to be rude but not wanting to encourage further talk, either, with the richest young man in town. His mansion loomed not far away.

For some odd reason Gasto had a crush on her, ever since the day they'd met several years ago at Freudendorf's spring festival. Though why he kept pursuing her, when every signal she gave made it clear she wanted nothing romantic to do with him, was beyond her.

He was as relentless and dumb as a donkey, and his pride knew no bounds. She couldn't stand the way he flaunted his wealth in people's faces.

"Looks like the beginning of a promising day, doesn't it?" Gasto flipped his head of lush toffee toned hair back, flexing his average shoulders as if they had muscle. His grin flashed long canines—a quirky genetic trait which all Freudendorf townspeople seemed to have.

Gasto fell into step with her, even as she tried to rush ahead. His long legs easily kept up. She clenched the book and basket tighter.

"A promising day, indeed," she said, leaving all emotion out of her voice. But it didn't seem to faze him.

"Yes, yes. It is as if autumn is promising the town a budding romance this year!"

Ugh, was that an attempt to make her think romantic thoughts and fall for him?

"Romance between, say, me and a certain beauty of lavender hair?" He hooked his arm around hers and gave a wink. She nearly gagged.

"You're thinking of spring. Autumn promises different things," she replied curtly. "Autumn brings the promise of cold and silence, withering life and gravestones, and stories that will haunt you during the full moon."

Gasto's mouth dangled open, so caught off-guard that he couldn't find words. His face could only make an awkward smile while his brain busied to find an answer.

Before he could recover, she freed her arm and turned toward the library.

He recovered and hurried after her.

"Autumn has more to offer than morbid things, I'm sure!" He jogged, hand reaching for her. "It's full of color and life, just like our relationship can be! Why, I could make all of your father's debts disappear in an instant, and give you all that your heart desires. I don't mind if you're missing half an arm—in fact, you seem quite capable despite it! Come, Rosenrot. Let us explore the romantic feelings we share for one anoth—"

She shut the library door behind her, blocking him out, holding the worn knob tight as he tried to jiggle it open from the other side.

She held her breath and waited, hand straining. From the desk, the librarian lifted a thick eyebrow at her. She flashed him a pleasant grin, to which he rolled his eyes.

Gasto's words were a muffled noise. "You'll come around, I know you will. There's nobody else more eligible to be your husband in this small town, than me," he went on. "I'll be waiting for you." He drew out the last word like a singing note, and she shuddered.

The tugging stopped, and footsteps pattered away.

She pressed her ear to the door.

He'd left. Finally.

She sagged with a sigh, letting out the stress, then turned to the rows of books for comfort.

"Should I dare ask?" came the old man's gruff question.

She shook her head with a nervous smile.

"Then I'll pretend you came back looking for a book you left behind," he commented. "My place isn't a lovers' hide-and-seek meadow, I hope you know."

Rosen ignored his grumble. The man enjoyed complaining and shooting snarky remarks, none to be taken seriously. She did, however, take time to browse further back into the library's rows—burning away an hour to make sure Gasto had really gone.

She soon found herself in the history section.

She let her fingers trail across book spines down the aisle. Worn fabric, smooth leather, bumpy scales—she savored the many textures. Her hand was stopped as it bumped into a book that'd been pulled halfway out. Curious, she took it out the rest of the way, and recognized the title: the book about Freudendorf history, the one that mentioned a castle and ruling family, and had inspired her as a tween to go out looking for it.

She closed the book and shoved it back. That memory still stuck with her—the unearthly wail, the wraith with glowing silver eyes—it had haunted her nightmares for many nights since.

A piece of her was still curious—the dangerous explorer who abandoned all reason piece of her. But she hadn't gone near the path up the western rising foothills since, the forbidden area that everybody knew of and nobody spoke of.

A book titled *Monsters & Beasts of Mythology* called for Rosen to pluck it off a shelf. She thumbed through depictions of furry beasts, fanged humanoids, and scaly creatures.

'The Nachzehrer, Beast of the Night…' she recalled. 'What was that creature I saw?'

The werewolf drawing looked too furry to be it, though the creature she had seen wore a cape.

A wraith, then? Possibly? It made more sense than anything else—well, as much sense as thinking you saw a mythological creature could be called sense.

The next page over depicted a vampire.

A revolted shudder jolted through her. Those creatures definitely did not exist. The dead could not come back to life as blood-sucking monsters. The very notion was idiotic! Her dead mother would never come back to life as some evil thing.

She closed the book, a bit too forcefully. She would sooner meet and chat with a wraith than a vampire. She wanted to slap sense into the people who enjoyed dressing up as vampires for the costume festival.

Rosen made her way out—Gasto nowhere in sight—back toward home with her basket.

The half-timbered apartment they lived in reminded her of sculpted gingerbread and icing on the outside, but inside it was a stuffy place packed with families, dusty air, and too-narrow stairs.

She teetered and creaked her way up the dim atmosphere to their door.

She smelled Dad before she saw him. Her nose cringed as she entered and spotted him sprawled down on the rug, a bottle of something beside his hand.

He grinned sluggishly up at her and tried to wave. "The girl's back!" he slurred. "Got some bacon 'n eggs to freshen up mah noggin' from all this buzz-buzzing? Won't leave mah ears, dernit!" He swatted his head as if at an insect, missing the target.

She stared down at his drunkenness. "Bacon? Who around here has that kind of luxury! We'll never be able to afford bacon, thanks to you."

"Now, now." He sat up, rocking side to side like an unsteady boat. "Does that be any way t' talk to yer good ol' father?"

"Good?" she scoffed and plopped the basket on the table.

It would be eggs and bread for every breakfast, lunch, and dinner this week.

THE DAYS CARRIED ON AS Rosenrot did odd jobs around town, earning however much money she could. Though there was plenty of work and repairs to be done, not all shops had the means to pay for it.

Old signs hung needing new paint, missing or crumbled pavestones tripped people; and while food and clothes still sold well enough, other shops were either having to limit their wares or close altogether.

Late afternoon found her sweating despite the autumn breeze while she trimmed the spindly evergreen hedges which fronted the largest residence in the valley. Her work was an interesting feat with one hand and an elbow that had become like a second hand to her from birth.

The wealthy Lord Kalt who ruled over the town dwelled here, at the very edge of Freudendorf on a hilltop. She didn't like it. It felt like the man was saying he was too good to dwell among the common folk.

Rosen watched as the lord's steam car rolled up the drive, stopping at the colonnaded front. Long, dark robes flowed around him, and a black beard trimmed to a point gave his features a sharp knife edge. Just watching him made goosebumps crawl up her skin. She cut away at another protruding branch.

She blamed the noble for the town's decline. He was supposed to be responsible for making them prosperous, but instead they lost more and more money with each passing year. If only the man would help put away the town's superstitious fear of the forbidden zone where the mines lay, they could begin mining salt again, and gain back the wealth that the history book once claimed Freudendorf had had.

It was sunset by the time Rosenrot made her way back home, and a letter waited for her in the dingy mailbox: a final warning notice. If Dad didn't pay off his debts to the money lenders soon, he would be jailed and everything they owned taken. It seemed the debt collectors had finally tracked Dad down.

Well, she could live with that. Let them take him and put him into labor to work off what he owed. She would sustain herself the same way she was now.

Inside the rented room, she tossed the letter at Dad's face. It bumped his nose before falling into his lap. He stared at it blankly as if it were some sort of alien.

She didn't bother explaining what was inside. She was exhausted from doing a day of real work and dragged her feet off to bed and the comfort of a lumpy pillow.

The loudest rooster in all the valley happened to be next door, and its warbling cry woke Rosen up with a start.

She tumbled out of bed, blinking at the light slanting in through the window. "That rooster needs some singing lessons," she muttered.

She scraped a brush through her short hair, pinned a small side braid, and slipped on her brown work dress and apron. Soon she had the eggs frying and plopped them onto plates. "Hey, wake up! Breakfast!" she shouted before sitting down to eat.

No sound answered her.

She chewed for a while, then grumbled and shouted again, "Breakfast! Get your lazy backside out of bed!"

Still nothing.

She shoved back her chair and marched into the bedroom. "I said, break—" She stopped short: The bed was empty.

Rosen craned her neck, scanning the room, then backtracked to the kitchen.

Dad wasn't anywhere.

Pulse pounding, she turned in place. Air from the drafty window flapped against something white—she picked up a piece of paper by the rug. It read:

Sorry to do this, girl, but I had to leave. The debt collectors are in town, coming to find me, so I'll be away for a few years. You're a hard worker; I know you can take care of the debt like a good lil' girl on your own. Take care!

There was a long pause as she stood there, staring open mouthed, before she crumpled the paper in newfound fury.

"*Ngrrrr!*" Her fist threw it hard out the opened window; it sailed like a missile. "You good-for-nothing!" she screamed.

A heavy knock on the door came suddenly. The sound filled her with dread.

She opened it to meet two pudgy, grim-faced debt collectors.

"*Guten morgen.* We've come for Mr. Hartmann," said one. He leaned in, peering about. "Although he doesn't seem to be here?"

They may have come for Dad, but Rosen was the only family member present, and therefore the one who had to take responsibility for his debts. That was the way of things, now.

"Take the furniture and whatever else my dad left here, but leave me be!" she said in vain, knowing what they would do next.

"Seeing as you have no means to pay the grievous debts, Miss Hartmann, you must do so with yourself. You are now the property of the debt collector's Guten Agency and will be sold into labor until all said debts are paid off." They chanted as one, as if the speech were given often.

Her jaw worked up and down, like a fish out of water, and before she knew it, she was being led down the narrow staircase and out the doors.

3

RosenRoT TReMBLeD, STaNDING IN line with the other unfortunates up on the platform, a rope pinning her arm to her side. A crowd of buyers was gathering. Soon to be sold into labor, she suddenly felt like a slave awaiting the end.

Rotten, rotten Dad! she growled inside her head as the selling began.

"Young man, 25 years of age, well-built. Ten years of debt to work off. Do I have a buyer?" hollered the auctioneer.

Buyers waved their arms, battling bids.

"Sold, to the gentleman in the green hat!" The auctioneer pointed.

Another man was auctioned off, and next a woman. And then…it was Rosen's turn.

Something started shuffling through the crowd clustered around the platform, something shabby, hunched and deathly green.

"Young woman, 18 years of age, a fine beauty if you dismiss the arm. Fifteen years of debt to work off. Do I have a buyer?" the auctioneer blared.

Rosen's toes squirmed inside her shoes.

A hand raised, belonging to an ugly toad of a man.

"15,000 marks for fifteen years! Do we have another offer?"

A second hand raised—a skinny, crooked man with an eel's grin.

Rosen shivered.

"15,500 marks! Going once…"

The first man shot his toad hand up again.

"16,000 marks!"

The crooked fellow sneered at the toady.

"Going once! Going twice! Going—"

Rosen stared grimly at her future: a toad man that would no doubt work her to death, and have her do who knew what else…

Why did this have to happen? Why did she have to end up stuck in this town of greedy people, abandoned by an awful parent?

"17,000 marks."

Rosen lifted her gaze at the creaky, strained voice, barely audible through the hubbub. A black sleeve with a greenish hand rose with the voice, and the frail arm shook as if the effort were too great. The owner was aged beyond humanly possible, with threads of hair jutting in all directions on a balding head. The old man made zombies seem like a real thing.

"17,000 marks from the old gentleman," hollered the auctioneer. "Going once! Going twice!"

The toady and the eel shot dreadful glares at the living corpse, who had suddenly swooped in and out-bid them. Thumbing through their wallets, the hammer fell before either one could bid again.

"Going thrice and sold! To the old gentleman!"

Rosen didn't have much time to contemplate if working for this zombie was a better fate than the toady. Hands grabbed and steered and shoved her down off the platform, toward the waiting hunchback form.

There was a ring of space around him as he signed two papers, as if everyone thought he looked too much like a zombie too, and the steering hands retreated from Rosen's back.

The whites of the old man's eyes were grayed, and Rosen tried not to stare at the dark splotches dotting his greenish complexion. At least he wore a suit. His bony, warty arm lifted, turned, and creaked in a gesture that meant "Please, after you."

She realized her arm had been freed from the rope.

With no other choice, she strode forward, and the zombie gentleman fell into step beside her, knee-joints popping.

They walked for over twenty minutes until they reached the edge of town. Rosen now followed slightly behind the old man, heading towards the single road that wound off through the valley and trees.

But the zombie man halted and turned to the right. With a shaky palm, he indicated an overgrown path veering to the side. His legs creaked and groaned as he took the forlorn path up a slope.

She peered up the path, trying to see where it snaked up to, into the western foothills. Surely nobody lived out there, so close to the forbidden zone, did they? She started after the old gentleman, catching up. Each footstep crunched through layers of autumn leaves. Birches stood white against the cacophony of orange and gold smothering the forest canopy. The sky was a sea of clouds, trapped by the mountaintops surrounding the valley, and growing darker by the minute, the fading light casting a strange glow and turning the autumn forest almost eerie.

"Where are you taking me?" Rosen asked tentatively, finally breaking the silence. "And why *me*?"

"I am…Butler Sterbetod." The old man's voice strained, like it was his dying breath, and she had to lean in to hear—though not too close; he smelled. "And…you are?"

"Rosenrot."

"Ah, Miss Rosenrot." His joints popped and wobbled. She thought a sudden breeze might blow him away. "I am…taking you to…serve Lord Varick."

Lord? There was another lord who lived around here, besides the creepy Kalt ruling town?

A branch covered in yellow leaves brushed the top of her head as she passed under. She reached and let her fingers graze along it fondly.

Hopefully, as a slave, she'd still be able to walk outdoors and soak in the beauty of nature.

"Lord Varick is in need of…a younger servant," Butler Sterbetod wheezed.

She creased her eyebrows. "And he has a home up in the mountains? To the west, where everyone's afraid to go?"

"The castle, yes."

Castle… She didn't know of any inhabited castle in the western foothills.

A rumble of thunder drew her gaze up to the frothing, grim clouds. The bright orange and yellow leaves were beginning to fade around them, melting away as dark trunks and red leaves took over.

A sea of red soon lined either side of the path. Twigs clawed down toward her from their bleeding canopy.

The memory rushed back: the path she had wandered as a too-curious girl. The wailing of a creature wrapped in black. Twin glowing silver eyes.

"The *forbidden* castle? Surely that isn't the one you're taking me to, is it?" She then repeated it louder, "Is it?"

Butler Sterbetod continued as if she hadn't stopped walking and cracked his neck back. "Forbidden? Hm...*ja*, it has been...a long time since...a human visited," he wheezed. "But it is...a nice place...to live. Much better...than with those other...gentlemen, I should think."

Well, on that she might agree. Living in a hole under a road would be better than living with any of those creepy buyers. But she knew nothing of this Lord Varick, or how he could live in a castle which none dared go near and all claimed to be cursed. Did he move here recently? He must have, to be so ignorant. The *Nachzehrer* was still rumored to dwell in these parts.

Rosen drew her cloak up to her chin against a breeze that should have been cold, but instead felt warm and moist. Strange. She considered turning around and making a run for it. Though she'd no doubt be caught and jailed for running away, and this butler would come for her again. Did she really have no other fate than this?

Loose leaves fell like drops of rubies around them. She caught one, and fingered a rotted hole, black along the edges. What if this Varick owned the Beast creature people were so afraid of, like some twisted kind of pet? Or what if he himself was the Beast?

She swallowed. *Whatever that thing I saw was, it wasn't human.*

DUKE GASTO THREW ON A shoulder cape and rushed out of his carriage, heading with a determined stride in his footsteps towards the auction platform in the center of town.

This was his moment, his chance! At long last, he could make the beautiful Rosenrot his!

Well, beautiful was an overstatement. But with a small town like Freudendorf, there weren't many options to choose from.

The moment he'd seen the news in the town paper that Rosenrot was to be sold, to pay off her family's debt, he had made his plan. He, the gracious and great Gasto, would come to her rescue. He would pay off her deft, and she would come live in his mansion, and there he would woo her, convince her that she belonged with no one other than his grand self, and she would finally fall for him.

"Rosenrot, my love!" He leaped like a merry deer and waved his hand high above the crowd gathered for the auction. "Your hero has arrived to save you!"

Heads turned his way, followed by scowls and grumblings. Gasto maintained his perfect smile, looking left then right, scanning the platform of people for lavender hair.

When he failed to find her, his hand made a fist and he demanded with a shout, "Where is the girl Rosenrot? I heard she was to be auctioned!"

"Yes, and so she was," the rotund auctioneer answered from his much higher stance on the platform.

Gasto grimaced at his air of superiority. "She *what*?" he exclaimed. "When? And *who* on earth to?"

"The signature on the contract reads to Lord Varick," the man read.

Gasto's expression froze somewhere between outrage and confusion. "To...who?"

Rosen's memory of the path into the forested foothills became more solid with each step. Butler Sterbetod led the way past a row of bushes and across a wide paved space. Up ahead loomed a gate.

This was the place where she'd seen the wraith. The bushes she had hid behind back then had either been trimmed or shoved aside to make walking room. She glanced left and right, making sure nothing lurked in the twisted, maroon undergrowth.

A burgundy vine wove and curled its tendrils around the dark rods of the ancient gate. The zombie butler clamped his hands around two rods, and it took his bony arms several yanks before the gate finally squealed open.

Beyond, rising and twisting into the stormy sky, stood a castle that embodied every sense of the word *forbidden*.

Vines like the one beside her climbed up stone faces. Gargoyles stared down from lofty perches on jutting turrets and arched window frames. The towers tipped with spires looked like fangs snarling at the world. Rosen tried to rub warmth into her limbs as she observed the unwelcoming aura of the castle.

Butler Sterbetod dipped his head and creaked his torso forward in a bow. "Welcome to Disteldorn Castle…Miss Rosenrot."

She dipped her head, feeling she ought to reply in some respectful way, even though every part of her wanted to turn tail and flee this growing nightmare.

She took tentative steps along a gravel path through the front courtyard, following the butler. Once-decorative plants in pots were black, wilted things, and the hedges were so uneven and overgrown it resembled a forgotten briar patch or a haunted maze. She tried not to trip on the roots of some thorny shrub winding its way through the gravel.

"So, I guess nobody cleans around here much?" she said sarcastically.

"The master prefers things…not to be disturbed," the butler replied in all seriousness.

Disturbed? As in, cleaned?

A set of stone steps, spotted with green moss and orange fungus, led to a set of grand arched doors: decorative rusted bolts running across a wood façade that had some rot. Whoever this lord was, he clearly didn't care about appearances—and to a rather lazy and pathetic extent.

His cleaning is certainly inhuman, she thought sourly.

The butler pulled and let drop a great rusted ring, which knocked on the door with a hollow thud. She waited behind his shoulder for something to happen, even though he was shorter than her.

The gargoyle above the door opened one stony eyelid.

Rosenrot held in a yelp. A glass eyeball turned and stared down at them, and then the eyelid shut.

There was a jostling of bolts on the other side before the door swung open.

Candle flames hovered in the open doorway, and someone spoke. "Oh my! This is the new servant? Welcome, welcome." A white smile flashed in the darkness. "And what is this lovely's name?"

Following Butler Sterbetod inside, it wasn't until Rosen's eyesight adjusted to the castle's dim atmosphere that she saw the hovering flames weren't attached to any candles, but rather were part of the wrists, elbows, ankles, and ears of a humanoid. No taller than her waist, his body was translucent like a thick layer of fog, yet somehow solid and wearing a gentleman's attire.

"Miss Rosenrot," answered the butler.

"How do you do, Miss Rosenrot?" said the person.

Rosen wasn't sure what to say. "Fine, I suppose, thank you."

"Pretty and polite, isn't she," he exclaimed. "How ever did this old geezer manage to convince you to come live and work here?"

She opened her mouth to speak, but then he waved his flame-wristed hand.

"No matter. I'm just glad you're here. We've been in need of a new face around these parts for quite some time." He chuckled. "And it's good that you don't get upset at the sight of nymiads. Some people, when they first see us, go into quite a panic, as if they've seen something dreadful. Can't understand why…" He shrugged his foggy shoulders. "We never hurt anybody, and we're talented at many things."

"Nymiads…aren't those creatures of folklore?" she asked tentatively.

"Ah, *ja*, we've been named in some ancient folklore. But none of what they say is actually true. It's just another fabrication to explain away the existence of Altered," he said.

"Altered?" Rosen recalled hearing a tale of once-humans who'd taken on strange forms and become something *else*, called the Altered, but she didn't know much else.

"Hm, I suppose most of us do prefer to stay out of the limelight, so to speak. It's no wonder you don't know of us. But anyhow!" Flames flapped as he waved his arm grandly. "You can call me Licht. Allow me to escort you to the master, *fraulein*—he's most likely in the drawing room."

Licht peered up at a grandfather clock to their right, wood as thick as a wardrobe and with a huge clock face that brushed up against the underside of a grand staircase.

"*Ja*, it's nearing lunch time." Licht stroked a hand through his jutting translucent hair. "Follow me, *fraulein*!"

Rosen clasped her hand to her other elbow in front of her, trying to mask the unease rippling through her stomach. She climbed up the curving staircase, following Licht's glowing flames. Nothing caught fire, even when Licht trailed his hand along the rail, as if the flames were of a different nature and under his control.

"What is Lord Varick like?" she found herself suddenly asking, wanting to fill the void while navigating the eerie, dim castle.

Licht and Butler Sterbetod shared a look.

"You didn't tell her?"

The butler's neck creaked as his head slowly shook.

"Well then." Licht brushed the sides of his thick-fog vest, mouth working, his teeth glowing as if flames hid inside them. "Varick is…is… How should I put it?" The nymiad made an effort to think.

"Difficult," Sterbetod wheezed.

"*Ja*. Extremely difficult." Licht nodded. "Try not to take anything he says to heart," he advised in a quiet tone.

Rosen glanced between them, her clasped palm getting sweaty. "Is he the *Nachzehrer*?"

Again the two shared a look. But Licht halted at a door before an answer could be given. "It'll be fine, I'm sure," Licht whispered, which didn't make her feel any better, then tapped on the door.

"Master Varick? The butler has arrived with the new worker you requested."

Several seconds of silence passed, and then faint footsteps could be heard drawing near, and the ornate door swung inward.

Dim light from the room beyond combined with Licht's flames to illuminate a figure standing tall in the doorframe.

Rosen's breath caught in her throat.

If a human could embody the words "dark prince" and "royal beauty," this was him. Perfect sharp nose and symmetrical features. Cat-like eyes and thick eyelashes black as night. Hair a dark waterfall cascading down in wavy layers brushing the tops of firm shoulders; his skin alabaster white. Lord Varick stared down at her, his irises catching the lamplight and glowing like silver coins.

"Master Varick, may I introduce Miss Rosenrot." Licht bowed with a wave of an arm and swirling flames.

Rosen made her best attempt at a curtsy, trying to halt the rapid beating in her chest. He was gorgeous. She didn't know a man could be called gorgeous.

His perfect lips parted to speak.

She held her breath, waiting for his elegant words.

"A human girl?" he said.

Rosen paused mid-curtsy. His tone didn't sound quite so pleasant as his appearance promised.

"I tell you to bring me a new nymiad servant—a male servant. A nymiad male servant. And instead, you bring me a human girl? A—human—girl?" His princely features distorted into a rude frown. "What is wrong with you, Sterbetod? Why can't you ever do things right!"

Rosen's jaw dangled, flabbergasted.

"But, Master…" Butler Sterbetod wheezed, one green hand over his chest. "A feminine touch will…do this castle good. She is a…hard worker, and…this place needs serious care or…else it will fall apart."

Varick's expression remained sourly unchanged.

"And I already…paid for her service…"

"You threw my money away on *that*?" The young lord pointed a long finger at her, no doubt taking in her half-missing arm.

Rosen snapped out of her daze. "Did you just refer to me as a *that*? Excuse me, but I am not a *that*."

"Shut up! Go away!" he shouted.

The door slammed in her face before she could finish.

She blinked at the polished wood, then turned her neck to look at Licht and the butler.

"Did he just—? Did he really—?"

"…Difficult," the butler concluded.

ROSEN RANTED AND RAVED. HOW could a lord behave in such a way? "Even street children have better manners! I won't stand for being treated like this—debts to be paid or not. They're not *my* debts, anyway. I'll run away and become a nun!" She huffed and puffed. "And what's he mean by *human*? Isn't he human, too?" she snapped at the air.

"You didn't tell her that part, either?" Licht eyed the butler, who gave a grin that lacked several teeth. "What *did* you tell her?" He tossed his arms in exasperation. Without waiting for an answer, the nymiad turned back to Rosen. "Let me explain, *fraulein*. Varick isn't human. He's—now, don't be alarmed when I say this—but he's…"

"Throwing another fit again?" a new voice interrupted.

Something shifted at the base of the staircase near Rosen, and she spun toward the voice, ready with a karate-chop hand raised.

A purple smile glowed and hovered in the air. "Master is the King of Fits. I doubt there's a soul in the world who could outdo him. If only it was something they gave medals for."

Licht came down the stairs to Rosen's side, and the light of his flames made the shadow nymiad visible.

The purple smile was attached to an angular face with long, pointed purple ears and a head of wispy black hair that moved as if underwater. Where Licht seemed to be made of solidified fog, this nymiad was made of dark shadows; thicker layers molded to resemble an old-style suit.

"This is Schatten," introduced Licht. "The other nymiad servant, besides myself, and quite the trickster."

"*Gasp*, I am an honest soul!" said Schatten, mock offended, but then he snickered. He took Rosen's hand, standing no taller than Licht. "A pleasure to have a new face around. I do hope you stay and don't let Lord Tantrum scare you away." He lifted off the ground, floating slowly up to better meet her height. Rosen realized Licht had been doing the same.

"If he's going to treat me like a splat of mud on his fine shoe, then I'm not hanging around," Rosen said, lifting her chin high.

"Oh don't be rash, young human." Worry flashed across Schatten's face briefly before he could hide it. "I'll go and have a chat with him. It could be that he's just in a rotten mood over something," he suggested. "Communication has always been a challenge for the young lord. He wasn't raised around people, you know."

He floated up the stairs.

"Communication?" Rosen snorted. "More like common decency and manners."

Licht moved to hover in front of her, as if afraid she might bolt for the exit doors. "Those things must be learned, *fraulein*—they are not present in anyone at birth," he told her. "Varick may be rough and unpolished on the outside," he gestured with his hands, wrist flames flickering, "But there's a soft spot inside him, I'm sure. He just needs…" Licht searched for the word, rolling his shoulders, and glanced to the butler for help, "…someone to bring that side out of him." He added a glowing smile, as if that could convince her.

"Not buying it," Rosen stated flatly.

"No compromise at all?" Licht struggled to keep ahead of her as she marched across the entry room toward the grand, rotting doors.

"Surely being a nun is a far worse fate?" The nymiad sounded desperate; in fact, they all seemed desperate for her to stay.

But why?

"All right," she said and stomped her boots to a halt. "If Lord Baby apologizes to me, then I'll stay."

Licht winced, and Butler Sterbetod sucked in a breath before coughing it out.

"I…" Licht held up a finger and paused. "I'll discuss it with him."

Shoulders bent inward and tense, he floated back up to the second floor.

"Master, you cannot live inside this bubble forever." Schatten gestured to the flaking walls surrounding the drawing room.

"I can do what I want. Shut up," said Varick.

"I don't mean you should leave the castle, Master, but

getting out and meeting new people would do you good. You might even make some friends!" encouraged Schatten.

"Friends. Why would I want those?"

"It could give you something fun to do—and teach you how to behave like a respectable person," Schatten muttered the last bit.

"What did you say?"

Schatten cleared his throat. "That girl, Rosenrot; why don't you start by befriending her?"

"She's a girl." Varick's fingernails dug into the wood of the table before him, its surface dusty and cluttered. "You know I can't have anything to do with a girl! This curse is…" He trailed off, and raised his fingers to look at them, then he gingerly touched the silver band encircling his neck. "Are you *trying* to ruin me?"

The accusation shot at Schatten like an invisible arrow.

"O-of course not, Master!" The shadow nymiad bumbled, trying to pacify his wrath. But Varick's wrath was not something to be so easily pacified. "We only want you to find some happiness and grow out of your shell. It's not like the girl is some poison you cannot go near."

"She is *exactly* that!" Varick slammed both palms on the table, rattling strewn bottles and books.

Schatten inhaled and clasped his shadowy palms together. "Deep calming breaths, Master—in and out." He motioned the breathing pattern, but Varick folded his arms and plopped down into his favorite princely plush chair, instead.

"Now," the nymiad continued, "nobody is saying you should like her, or fall in love or anything heinous—none of us wants that. We are well aware of your curse, Master. We know how much you would miss your handsome appearance should any…*romantic* feelings take hold and activate said curse."

Varick tilted his chin to a small wall mirror. "Yes, I would miss it sorely." He brushed his finger down his jawline. "What would be the point of living if I was ugly? Beauty has meaning, ugly does not." His long fingers snatched a pumpkin crumpet from one of the bowls on the table and popped it into his mouth. "That girl, for example," he continued. "How does she live with herself? She's a weak human, to begin with." He shuddered in disgust. "And that hair is so...frizzy." He wiggled his fingers in the air to demonstrate. "But lacking a hand—*a hand!*—if that doesn't spell ugly, then I don't know what does." He munched a second sweet crumpet. "How does she find the will to live?"

Schatten tensed. "Perhaps you should ask her, yourself?"

In that moment Licht strode into the room, his manner hovering between pleading and demanding. "Master, that was no way to treat a lady. If you don't apologize soon, she'll leave!"

"Lady? If persons like that can be considered a lady, then I'm glad for this curse." Varick crossed a leg over his knee. "Let her leave. Such unsightly features put a smudge on my castle. And why is she so chubby in the chest? It's weird."

Schatten looked toward Licht, who face-palmed. "I suppose this is your first time seeing a female other than your mother," Licht said quietly. "You do remember those anatomy books I had you read, yes?"

"No. Nor do I care to."

Licht paused for a second, then pushed the matter aside. "Well, we can have a talk about that later. But for right now, go apologize to her. We need her here. You need her here. Another person who's your age, and who *at least* resembles your race better than we nymiads do."

"If a friend is what you wanted to get me, then why wasn't it a male?" Varick snapped bitterly, crumbs spilling over his lips.

"Sterbetod tried his best. And anyway, it's too late to change things now," Schatten reasoned. "You don't want 17,000 marks to go to waste, do you?"

"Seventeen-thou—!" Varick's eyebrows contorted. "He spent *that* much?"

"Apologize, and put Rosenrot to work, or all of that will have been wasted," Licht finished.

There was a vile taste in Varick's mouth, and he reached for a glass of pumpkin-flavored water. "Seventeen-thousand…fine! Bring the human here."

Rosenrot crossed her arms—well, one and a half arm—but finally followed Licht back upstairs to the drawing room. This had better be a good apology, or it was off to the nuns for her!

The door opened, and as she stepped inside, a strong scent of pumpkin overwhelmed her senses. Hand to her nose, she scanned the drawing room and its dark furnishings, all the fabrics of orange hues. The princely chair Lord Varick reposed in was stark black wood and orange upholstery.

She didn't want to look directly at the man, and focused instead on the bookcases and shelves, lined in cobwebs and holding strange collections of mushrooms growing in terrariums.

"Do you have a name, girl?"

She did her best not to throw the nearest bowl of crumpets at him. She snatched one and plopped it in her mouth. Pumpkin flavored? Was everything in here pumpkin?

"I should hope every person has a name. Mine is Rosenrot," she replied.

Varick propped his elbow on the chair arm and touched his thumb to his chin and first two fingers to his temple—like a prince looking down on his subject. This time, she noticed a cape around his sharp shoulders.

"Rosenrot, Rrrosen rrrot…" He rolled the name about. "Miss Rot, I trust you understand the value of money and what it means when labor has been paid for? If you leave this castle, it will be as a thief, and I will have you hunted down and jailed for stealing from me."

Licht sucked in his lips, and Schatten mumbled something to the air.

Was this supposed to be an apology? Rosen pressed her elbows against her sides.

"I am not a thief, Lord Vak. I came willingly to do the labor you paid for," she said. "I can clean, trim the plants, wash windows, but what I will *not* do is let someone treat me as if I'm less of a person than they are."

One of his perfect eyebrows lifted.

"I will work for you, but I will not be treated as a *that*," Rosen finished.

"Vak?" The lord's perfect lips pouted. Then his eyelids closed and his nose turned away. "Whatever. As long as you do your work, you can eat and wear what you like, and choose any bedroom. That should be enough for you, yes?" He twirled his fingers in the air, and plucked another pumpkin crumpet.

Rosen's mouth twisted to the side.

Did he understand a word of what she'd just said? His behavior was despicable!

The shadow nymiad did mention that Varick hadn't been raised around people. Judging by the cobweb décor of this room, and no doubt every room, it did seem that he lived alone.

"You can start with the windows. Light doesn't shine through them the same as it did before dust settled in." Varick buffed his nails on his vest and inspected their shine. "Sterbetod's too old for the job, now."

Rosen didn't bother to curtsy before she left. A flash of red caught her eye: Now that his gorgeous face was too aggravating to look at, she noticed a necklace around his neck: a gothic band of metal with a rose at its center made of raw ruby gem petals. Each of the petals glowed with an inner light.

"Are those real rubies?" she murmured.

Varick's eyelids popped open; the look he gave her was hunted and suspicious, his hand clutching the ruby rose from her sight.

The sudden change made her flinch, and she saw her way out the room.

How many windows did a castle have?

"I guess I'll find out," she mouthed.

6

THE STORM THAT HAD THREATENED to burst during Rosen's hike to the castle now launched its assault upon the valley, lightning slashing the clouds purple, thunder rumbling the foothills.

She watched through the window glass as she scrubbed it clean, the rise and fall of the land and forest beyond buffeted as the wind gusted and tossed leaves high, swirling bouquets of red.

Ten windows done.

She dropped the washrag in a bucket. Already her hand ached. She switched to her left elbow—it could push the rag over the glass but couldn't reach high.

Feee…feee…

Rosen's ears perked, and she twisted to look over her shoulder. The wispy sound came like a note from a flute, only no one was there.

Something red vanished around a corner.

Rosen dropped the rag again and crept toward the corner, her unquenchable curiosity awakened.

Reaching the corner, back pressed against the wall, she rounded it quickly with her chopping hand raised.

Red flickered and vanished…flickered and vanished…down the dark corridor beyond.

Lowering her hand, she followed, footsteps muffled on an expensive, dilapidated carpet stretching into the shadows.

Feee…

Rosen raced to catch up, squinting to keep the red glow in her sight, flickering like a firefly. It veered left, and she skidded, catching herself on a doorframe. The red flicker had flown through the open door.

She sucked in a breath then peeked inside, taking one cautious footstep at a time. The room was dim; she could make out the shape of a large canopy bed and some other furnishings. Heavy drapes and the bad weather outside made the dust-encrusted windows barriers to any sunlight. She should clean them up, then get a proper look at this room.

Red flickered in the corner of her eye, and she turned, coming face to face with a woman.

"Eek!" Rosen covered her mouth. A flash of lightning managed to glow through one window and reveal the gilded frame of a painting. The face was a painting—not real.

Rosen breathed. The fair woman seemed to be staring down at her, swathed in red ruffles and frills. Goosebumps crawled up Rosen's arm.

The next painting over had a gentleman who seemed to watch her every move, his top hat and cane stately and somehow familiar. Had she seen him before, somewhere? The style reminded her of old photographs in books. In history books… Oh, that's where she'd seen him!

That book about Freudendorf's history had several gray-and-white photographs. And this man—though depicted much older here—had been in one of them.

"Are these Varick's relatives? They certainly look wealthy, a lord and lady."

Could they be the family who'd once ruled the town, long ago, before that creepy Lord Kalt took over?

Fee-ee!

The red firefly hovered by the door now, and something metallic squealed in protest before a lamp burned to life on the wall. The red thing perched on the lamp's knob, and Rosen blinked. It had the head of a red thistle flower, and spindly, sharp limbs made of thistle leaves. A line that was its mouth curled up, and glossy leaves for eyes watched her draw near.

"What are you?" she asked.

"Our resident pixit—a very mischievous species, I should warn you. You probably know them better as pixies." Licht appeared in the doorway. "Need a break, Miss? I doubt Master meant that you should clean every single window in one evening. Eh…" He glanced about. "Especially not these windows. The master would throw more than a tantrum if anything were to be disturbed in his parents' bedroom."

"Are those his parents?" She pointed to the two paintings.

Licht shook his head, the flames of his ears swishing. "His grandparents. These"—he strode over to the other wall—"are his parents."

The single painting depicted an elegant couple, their hair the same luscious black as Varick's, and skin just as pale. There between them, very small, was a young boy with silver eyes and a smile hovering on his lips. It had to be Varick, though the boy in this painting felt different: peaceful, enthusiastic and happy—as if the world had so much to offer, so much that he wanted to explore.

She felt a shudder. It reminded her of her childhood self, before cold reality of a lost mother and a useless father settled in.

What cold reality had wiped off that peaceful smile from Varick?

"Dinner will be soon. We may as well give you a tour around the castle, beforehand." Schatten's purple smile glowed from out of the shadows to join them.

Fee, fe-ee!

"Must you tag along?" Schatten frowned as the pixit poked at his long purple ears, and he swatted his hand.

"Be nice, you two." Licht pushed Schatten out the door and motioned to her. "Come, Miss Rosenrot."

"Ouch! Don't touch me!" Schatten turned in the corridor, trying to massage his back. "I told you not to touch me with those flaming hands!"

"Wrists, not hands. And I can't help it—they don't snuff out, you know."

"You can control those flames, and you know it! Maybe I should keep a bucket of water on hand," the shadow nymiad muttered.

Fee-heehee!

"Now that's just mean," said Licht. "Stop laughing, Fee."

The pixit giggled, leaves rattling, and flew to land on Schatten's shoulder.

"Ouch! Those thistle thorns hurt!"

Rosen followed them up the corridor, a piece of her reluctant to leave the painting and its ghost image of a once happy family behind.

The castle was a maze of narrow corridors, tall windows, wide rooms that led into rooms which then led into *more* rooms—and all decorated in the most lavish, gothic affair. Any bright colors, tapestries and fabrics had faded or worn, and the elegant dark-wood furnishings were layered in years' worth of dust. The niches, rails, columns and ribbed ceilings were hidden in cobwebs. She touched a green glass vase, displayed on a corridor table, and balked at the layer of white stuck to her fingertip.

This place was more like an abandoned haunted mansion—the kind in grim fairytales—though the remnants underneath begged her to believe it wasn't always so. She flinched as a floorboard creaked unstably under her weight.

The shadow nymiad waved here and there as they toured, announcing rooms and what they were used for: the kitchens, the boiler, the many guest corridors, the servants quarters, and so on and so on. "And this"—Schatten faced her before a set of doors, thistles and thorns carved decoratively about the wood—"is the library!"

Dust bunnies fled as the doors whooshed open.

Rosen's jaw dropped and her feet carried her forward. "This is my happy place," she whispered to the air, tilting back her head to stare at the rows upon rows upon rows of shelves and floor levels and spiral staircases reaching to the ceiling. A world of books, a wonderland of every form of literature ever to have graced the lands.

Rosen drew in a deep breath through her nose, the old sent of leather, fabric covers, and paper filling her senses, her being.

This was paradise.

She could die happy now.

"I try keeping this place clean, but...well." Licht blew the dust off a table and a book on display. "Flames don't do well near paper, even if I can control them." He waved his wrists and elbows.

Schatten rolled his eyes. "Excuses. I told you I'd trade you the boiler room for this one. The boiler is much more your style."

"I hate the boiler! It's hot and unfriendly, not open and bright, like this."

Massive windows ran up the floor levels, letting in more light than anywhere else in the castle. The fading storm outside had left the sky gray.

"So you force *me* to be stuck with it?" Schatten glowered. "That does it! I'm doing the library from now on!"

"No, Miss Rosen is." Licht gestured toward her. "I think she's already fallen under its enchantment."

"Fine." Schatten lifted his shoulders. "But you're taking on the boiler room for two months!"

Licht's translucent face made an exclamation.

Just then, a stomach growl echoed through the library. Rosen pinched her lips, face red. "Is it time for dinner yet?"

Thankfully the dining table, and most of the burgundy-themed dining room, had been cleaned. Licht ushered Rosen to the seat at the end of the table—Lord Varick already seated at the opposite end and brooding. He shot a glare across the space as she sat, then frowned down at the empty placemat.

"What is taking the chef so long?" His growl became a whine. "Did I march all the way in here just to sit before an empty table and stare at a crippled human?"

"Crippled?" Rosen's hackles lifted.

"No, Master, of course not. I'm sure it's on the way, any moment now," Licht replied with a tremble in his voice.

"I may be missing half an arm, but that doesn't make me a cripple," she said leaning forward, and glared across the table, palm pressing on the wood.

"Doesn't it?" He stared point-blank in return. "Don't you find certain tasks difficult? Or can you wield that fork in your mouth while your hand uses the knife to cut?"

Rosen looked down at the silverware. It was a struggle to use a fork and knife at once.

Was this Varick really the same sweet, cheerful boy from the painting? That boy would never have been so rude and unfeeling!

The back doors swung open and in creaked Butler Sterbetod, with a rolling cart and trays. The cart bumped into the table before his popping wrists could stop it.

Varick pinched his brow between two fingers. "You're giving me a headache, Sterbetod!"

"Yes, Master...sorry, Master..." The butler's shoes shuffled along the carpet as he picked up the first tray and carried it over. The dishes rattled, and Rosen feared he might drop it, but somehow the zombie-like butler made it over and plopped the tray onto the polished table.

Sterbetod's hands shook the platter of beef and giant bowl of soup as he filled their plates and bowls, contents barely managing not to spill over the sides. Varick frowned disdainfully, watching the process until his dinner was set on the placemat before him. He raised his knife and fork.

Sterbetod creaked and groaned back towards the tray, but Rosen rushed over and retrieved her dishes herself, sparing the elder man the effort. "Oh, Miss...you don't have to..."

She waved it away, coming back to pick up her soup bowl.

Varick watched her as he sliced his slab of beef, using the knife a little too obviously, a ghost smirk in the crease of his lips.

She sat down harshly and picked up the knife with her hand, then pressed the fork's handle with her dexterous elbow: pressing the fork into the beef, to keep it in place while she sliced. The knife wasn't very sharp, but she sliced up the beef and then took the fork in hand to eat.

Varick regarded her utensil work, while he spooned down an orange colored soup.

Satisfied with her accomplishment, Rosen tasted the soup—pumpkin soup, of course. "You have a thing for pumpkin, don't you?"

His glare shot back up, though he continued spooning down soup. "Do you have something against pumpkins?" he asked in a threatening tone.

She shrugged. "I like them just fine."

His glare mellowed a fraction, and he looked away with a snort.

The pumpkin soup was delicious—then again, anything other than eggs and cheap bread was. She finished every scrap and crumb of dinner, even lifting the bowl to lick it clean—she'd never had such wonderful food in all her poverty-stricken life!

Disgust and approval warred on Varick's features. He clapped his hands, and Sterbetod brought in dessert: slices of decadent pumpkin cake topped with icing.

Oh my, she could eat like this every day! Maybe putting up with Varick was worth it—especially considering that library paradise.

"Ah, the weather is clearing up!" Schatten entered, taking up their finished plates, despite the butler's protest that he could manage. "We didn't show you the gardens yet, Miss Rosenrot," he said, floating to the cart and setting the tray down. He half turned toward the lord, his hair moving as if touched by an unfelt breeze. "Perhaps Master would care to join us? Get a breath of fresh air, and show the miss how you'd like the plants to be trimmed?"

Varick shot him a withering look before wiping a napkin across his perfect lips. He rose and stomped towards the door, glossy hair jostling around his proud cheeks. "I might venture into the gardens, since I feel like it," he stated without looking. "You should know, though: I'm picky about how I want the gardens to look."

He donned a black velvet cape as he left.

Rosen stood and followed reluctantly, Schatten urging her on. Down the grand staircase, and through a corridor, a squeaky door led out onto a marble patio. From there, the gardens sprawled.

It was in the same sorry state as the front courtyard—gravel paths overgrown with thorny weeds and choking vines, hedges and bushes misshapen, twisted trees looking like gothic beings. She took a moment, head dizzy. How was she supposed to fix all of this?

Thunder rumbled, a faint echo as the storm retreated over the mountains, leaving behind an overcast sky that barely let evening light glow through.

"I should grow a pumpkin patch," Lord Varick stated. He posed beside her, hand on his hip, surveying the gardens as if they were lush and not about to crumble into pieces.

"Uh-huh…" Rosen eyed him sidelong.

Nose high, Varick marched down the patio steps, spreading his arms wide before the gardens. "My beautiful domain. So many new vines have grown!"

Rosen cast a glance at Schatten, who shrugged blankly. She followed Varick into the overgrown, creepy paths.

Varick's fingers caressed the tendrils of a mass of interwoven vines, which were smothering a stone bench and its companion angel statue. "Yes, so lovely," he cooed.

Rosen tried not to let her face show what she was really thinking.

"A little trim on the dead ends should help them," he told her, his focus on the vines. Next were the twisted, decorative trees. "Just enough pruning to keep them healthy and thriving—no changing their shapes, mind you."

"So…you want a garden that's made of vines, thistles, and misshapen flora?" she asked.

He shot a pouting look over his shoulder. "They're beautiful. Can't you feel the lonely, forgotten aura they give off? So distant and forlorn, it's almost magical."

He knelt to the patches of thistles filling in what should have been flower beds. "Thistles have the most exquisite shape, like twisted roses. Their alluring flowers draw you in, and their thorns steal your blood. Yet they do not last for long, no matter how hard they struggle to survive. They soon wither away and must leave this world behind. It's truly romantic."

Rosen made a face at his back, then quickly hid it when he turned. "Thistles are pretty, in their designated place," she agreed, and touched the tip of a purple flower puff. "Roses are my favorite, though."

"Hm, makes sense. It matches your name," he said and moved on.

The way he described flowers and thorns—alluring yet dangerous—was almost poetic, she had to admit.

They reached rows of trellises; a few rose buds still bloomed along the rafters despite the autumn chill. He touched one bud that was wilting black. "Such a fleeting life…"

He stared at the petals, as if seeing through them to something in the past. His other hand went subconsciously to the ruby rose necklace at his neck.

Rosen wet her lips and asked, "Your ancestors, are they the ones who used to rule the town in the valley?" She nodded beyond the castle, where the steep foothill they were on dropped down toward the valley.

"Yes." He seemed reluctant to say it.

"Do you ever think about buying the town back and becoming the governing force?" she asked. "The town could use someone new, someone more open to advancement."

She paused.

Varick wasn't exactly the picture-perfect lord for the job…but beggars couldn't be choosers.

"I want nothing to do with the outside world," Varick snapped. "Lord Kalt is doing just fine."

"Oh, so you know of him?"

"Of course I do. Why are you prying into my business?" His silver eyes glared darkly.

"I saw the painting—the one of your…parents." She took a step back.

"That has nothing to do with you. Stay out of my business!" Varick stormed past her, cape swishing. "Human greed knows no bounds…" he muttered harshly.

Rosen turned after him. "Why do you keep referring to me as a human? You're human too, aren't you?"

Varick barked a laugh and halted.

Rosen clenched her hand. "Are you the one I saw, all those years ago? Wrapped in a cape, crying and screaming at the night sky?" she demanded to know, gathering her nerves. "Are you the one they call *Nachzehrer*, Beast of the Night?"

Varick turned so that one silver eye met hers. "And if I say that I am, what will you do? Scream in terror and flee? The *Nachzehrer* is said to be a vampire beast, you know."

Rosen pressed her shaking hand across her stomach. "The dead do not come back to life. Vampires cannot exist."

Varick turned all the way around until he faced her. "Is that so?"

He drew one step nearer, a shaft of evening light appearing through the clouds and spilling over him, glinting off his eyes, his teeth. Off his perfectly twin set of fangs, masked previously by the castle's darkness.

"Nobody bothered to inform me that I could not exist." He pulled out a hidden knife from his jacket and sliced it across his arm.

The cut bled, then healed itself before her.

Rosen started back with a sharp gasp, her hand catching herself on the wing of an angel statue. She moved to keep the statue between them.

This couldn't be real—vampires weren't real! But what her mind thought and what her eyes were seeing contradicted. In a flurry of panic, Rosen ran.

She ran for the garden gate, metal squealing as her hips shoved through.

"Going somewhere?" Varick appeared off to the side, catching up with her in an instant.

She screamed and launched herself over a prickly hedge. Hitting the ground on the other side, jarringly, she rolled to her feet and bolted into the forest surrounding the castle.

The ground sloped before her. She could hear Varick leap over the hedge as she hurried across the leaf-strewn ground, twigs clawing at her skirt. The sun dipped below the tops of the mountains, plunging the forest into near darkness.

Her left foot missed ground, sinking through a depression made of piled rotting leaves, and she lost her balance—falling sideways, striking her side and tumbling down the steep decline.

The world became a flurry of soil and foliage as she rolled helplessly, her single hand useless to stop herself, tumbling down the side of the mountain.

Her right ribs crashed into something, and her falling halted. A wave of leaves smothered over her like an avalanche set loose.

And then, all was silent, but for a distant night bird.

She breathed, in and out, pain like fire in her side.

Well, at least this was better than being bled dry by some vampire. She could die happy in a forest, as long as no carnivore found her first.

If only it were daylight, though, so she could see the pretty forest colors. Autumn was the time for sorrow and morbid things—it would make a nice requiem for her death.

Rosen let her eyelids close.

7

ROSEN FELT ARMS LIFT HER, carry her. The crunch of leaves underfoot echoed in her ears.

"Master, how could you do this?" someone berated. "Do you not realize how fragile humans are? If she doesn't survive this…"

"Enough! I'll handle it," said a deeper voice.

Rosen's back rested against something soft as she was laid down. Her eyes opened a fraction, the dim light of candles and a fireplace letting her see the room.

Hands slid under her back to undo the zipper of her dress.

With a cry of alarm, she sat up and struck foreheads with someone. Between the new headache, and the fire pain in her side, she started to cry.

"Ow." The someone was Varick, and he rubbed at his forehead grumpily. "Don't sit up; you'll make it worse," he ordered.

"You evil monster!" she yelled.

His brow creased and lips thinned. "Humans. Always judging what they don't understand... If anything is *evil* around here, it's your kind."

He noticed the tears running down her cheeks, and his temper softened. He glanced away, suddenly flustered. "Just stay still and let me heal you, all right? Your ribs are fractured."

He reached to unzip her dress and she jerked away on the plush settee. "How can I heal your ribs if I can't touch them?" he said with a scowl.

Rosen tried to speak, but only tears and a sob came out.

Varick rose from the chair he'd pulled over and threw up his hands. "What am I supposed to do?"

Licht entered the room, the flames on his wrists, ears and joints dancing. "Perhaps the chef can help?" he suggested, and stepped off to the side as a figure approached:

It was an old woman, with skin like bark and clothes made of leaves and moss. Layers of moss formed a chef's apron. She came up to the settee and patted Rosen's arm.

"Hello, Rosenrot. I am Mrs. Moos. Come, let me help you out of that dress." Moos turned to the lord. "Master, I suggest you reflect upon your behavior and how poorly you've treated this young woman. My, look at the distressing state you've put her in!"

She shooed the men with her bark hands. "Go out, scoot. I'll call you when we're ready."

Varick's shoulders lifted to his ears sulkily; Licht tugged on his hand and led him outside.

Mrs. Moos turned back to Rosen. "Now then, let's get

things situated. Do dry your eyes, dearie. This whole day must have been quite a shock for you."

Rosen dabbed her eyes with a napkin. Shock felt like an understatement. She couldn't move much from the pain, but the moss woman was dexterous and soon had Rosen in a loose shirt and pants, the muddy dress taken away to be cleaned. Mrs. Moos called Varick back inside, "You can heal the miss, now."

Varick strode into the room, for the first time wearing a simple white dress shirt and no cape. Rosen wanted to run, but even trying to sit up lanced pain through her side.

"Don't you worry, dearie. You'll be good as new in no time!" Mrs. Moos shuffled off with Licht. Rosen opened her mouth to beg the moss woman to stay, but she didn't want to sound desperate, and Moos vanished before she could think any further.

Varick took his seat in the chair before the settee, and Rosen eyed him with apprehension. The ruby rose around his neck reflected firelight, yet also seemed to glow from the inside.

He leaned forward and placed his hand to her injured side under the shirt, his touch surprisingly gentle. His eyes closed, and a cold sensation like ice cubes spread along her ribs beneath his hand. His brow furrowed in concentration. "It's only a fracture, thankfully, or this would be much more difficult," he murmured; she wasn't sure if it was to her or himself.

Rosen didn't know what she expected the healing to be, except salves and strange medicines. But instead the *Nachzehrer* was beside her, touching her skin and somehow healing her ribs. A vampire was touching her.

Her lower lip trembled and her hand shook, but she didn't dare move yet—who knew what the being might do.

"I...apologize for frightening you." Varick hung his head, not meeting her gaze, like a guilty child. Rosen watched him.

He glanced up at her face briefly. "I didn't mean for you to get hurt. I'm not used to fragile creatures such as humans." He lifted his hand—her ribs knit solidly back together, the skin unbruised.

"Are you...well?" he asked.

Rosen blinked. Was this the same person who had been throwing tantrums?

She nodded to his question. He licked his thumb and brushed it across a cut on her arm. The cut healed as she watched.

He touched several other cuts on her wrist and palm. Her hand was still shaking and he must have felt it.

"Do they really call me Beast of the Night?" he asked, focused on her hand.

Rosen swallowed. If she said yes, would it throw him into another angry fit?

"They don't even know me, yet they judge me," he mumbled.

"Can you blame them? You live alone in this creepy castle, and at night you howl to the sky." She knew she shouldn't have said it, but her mouth had a habit of speaking before she could think.

He met her gaze then, eyes liquid silver. "I do not howl to the sky," he said firmly. "That was years ago, and I was..."

She waited, but he didn't finish. "Crying?" she said for him.

He glared at her.

"It's okay to cry," she hurried on to say. "Everybody cries. I cry too, obviously." She looked down at her lap sheepishly.

Varick lifted his hand, setting it against her right temple, fingers brushing through her hair as his thumb drew above her right eyebrow. "Another cut," he said when he noticed her wide-eyed stare, and he quickly withdrew his hand.

Rosen's heart thumped in her chest. "Why were you crying, that night long ago?"

His mouth opened, and then his face turned away. "Herbal tea is waiting for you—Mrs. Moos says it will help calm your nerves." He rose to leave.

"Lord Varick," she said suddenly, and he paused at the door. "I'm sorry for judging you so quickly. I hope you won't judge me, likewise, for being human?"

After a moment, he smirked. "I suppose I can try."

Varick lounged in the chair before the fireplace of his living quarters, swirling a glass of *apfelschorle* and staring into the fire glumly.

"Master, you're soon going to dowse the fire with that broody expression of yours," said Schatten, while he put away the lord's clean clothes. "Why so down? Is it something to do with Miss Rosenrot?"

Varick grumbled and crossed his legs.

"You know, Master, there'd be no harm in being friends with her. I know you fear love, what with the curse and all, but simple friendship should be a safe thing for you. And I think you'd rather enjoy the company of someone closer to your age and form." Schatten hid a sly grin.

Varick tapped his temple, thinking over the nymiad's words.

Friendship. Maybe it could work. It would be nice to have a friend, like the kind he read of in novels. Every main character had a friend at their side. Someone to share secrets with, go off on adventures with.

Adventures...he had never stepped foot beyond the mountains and had an adventure before. He wondered what the outside world was like.

Rosen woke to the early dawn in a plush bed, surrounded by silk and downy-feather blankets. She blinked at the canopy above the bed, ruffles of lavender silk.

She rose and padded over to one of the windows in her designated bedroom. Beyond, clouds of fog pooled between the mountainsides and foothills, making the tops of land resemble floating islands of trees in a sea of white.

"Licht! Schatten!!"

Varick's voice blared through the castle walls.

Rosen creaked her door open a fraction.

"What's wrong, Master?" came Licht.

Varick stormed out of what Rosen guessed was the shower room, wearing nothing but a towel. "The shower stopped working again! How am I supposed to rinse my hair?"

"Oh my, the pipes must have begun leaking again. If only we could hire a proper plumber," said Licht.

"I tried," said Schatten. "None are brave enough to come to the forbidden castle—and those were the few who didn't run screaming when they saw a nymiad, in the first place."

"Oh, my beautiful hair," Varick moaned. "It's going to get oily and gross. I don't want to live anymore."

Rosen snorted.

Schatten threw up his hands and muttered to himself, something about being spoiled.

"Master, one day without a wash isn't going to hurt you. Go get dressed, and we'll have the pipes working again by tonight," Licht encouraged.

Rosen peeled herself away from the sight of Varick's sleek, bare torso, half of her amused and the other half blushing.

She searched through the wardrobe in her room, finally pulling out a blue dress that wasn't as frilly as the rest.

Breakfast was a spread of fresh bread, sausages, and soft-boiled eggs perched in porcelain egg cups.

"I need you to dust my drawing room," said Varick. He self-consciously had his hair back in a low ponytail.

Rosen chewed her lip not to laugh. Being poor, showers had never been a daily luxury for her, and she often had to use whatever river or pond she could find. She doubted Lord Varick could stomach doing such a thing.

"Don't touch the cobwebs, though. Some are decorative," he added.

She gave him a look. He was worried about bathing, yet fine with cobwebs? "So, you just want me to clean off the dust?"

"That's right."

"Okay. That makes no sense," she mumbled to herself when she stood, finished eating.

She wasted no time and brought several dustrags into the orange-upholstered drawing room, and surveyed the work needing done. Dust made cake layers on the shelves, and there were a lot of shelves. How could he breathe in this room? Or did he need to breathe?

She got to work dusting with feathers first, then cloths. The numerous terrariums growing mushrooms were in the way, and with only one hand, she couldn't lift them easily.

Varick peeked his head through the doorway. "Is it going well?"

He sounded nervous. She looked back at him. But of course, this was his favorite room and his treasured collection of mushrooms.

"I haven't destroyed anything, if that's what you mean," she shot back. "But I could use help dusting under these terrariums. Lift them for me, will you?"

Varick crossed the floor, his footsteps barely making a sound. He lifted a wide, rectangular terrarium growing a tree branch covered in various green mosses and clusters of purple mushrooms in soggy soil.

"Purple; those are pretty," she said.

"*Laccaria amethystine*. It loves the forest and dampness," he said, marveling at their color as he held the glass case. At first she shied from how close he stood, but then he stepped to the side.

She still wasn't sure what to think of him being a vampire—or whatever he was. He didn't quite fit the mold of what she'd expected. Pale as he was, he seemed full of life, and the sunlight didn't burn him.

The next specimen was a round glass sphere containing wide, shiny green mushrooms with pale stems and white speckles, growing in wood-chip mulch. "*Stropharia aeruginosa*; it's very much enjoying the autumn season. I should water it some more, though."

He inspected several other terrariums while Rosen cleaned, and he pressed a finger to his temple. "Some of these need replacing… I'll have to go out hunting today."

Rosen's dustrag paused. "Hunting mushrooms?"

He glanced her way. "You can come along, if you wish. I could use an extra set of hands—erm, hand." He looked away. "If you don't find mushrooms boring, that is."

Rosen finished the last shelf. "I find them interesting. They're like nature's little hidden gems," she said.

Varick's lips almost rose to smile. "Good, then I'll fetch you a basket."

Fog lingered in the forest as Rosen followed Varick up the mountain slope near the castle. Spruces filled the air with their earthy spice scent. The hem of her cloak brushed along the leaf-mulch ground behind her.

She carried a woven basket matching Varick's, and where the slope leveled out a bit, they spread out, beginning their hunt. "Collect one of every different color you find," he instructed her.

A rust-colored mushroom forced its cap through the fallen leaves at the base of an oak. "I found one!" she shouted.

Varick hurried over. "Excellent. Take the trowel and dig deep, all around and underneath the mushroom, without disturbing it much."

He showed her, carving out the patch of dirt before lifting the trowel up under the mushroom. "The spores are what we really want. Mushrooms are simply the flowers that the spores bloom. So, to grow more mushrooms, you need to collect the spores."

She edged away from his closeness slightly. "I can't see them."

"No, spores are too small to see." He placed the chunk of soil with its gem into one of the cloths in his basket, and tied it closed. "And that's how you do it!" he finished, pleased. "For any mushrooms that are attached to trees, just peel the bark free, or better yet, cut the section of wood off."

Rosen went to work, scanning the forest floor, feeling like a wolf on the prowl. The air moistened her skin, and the overcast light made the colors of nature stand out deeper, richer. Acorns crunched underneath her boots.

A row of white mushrooms grew out of the side of a

dead tree, shaped like oysters, without stems. She pried around the bark and lifted chunks off, setting them in a cloth with care.

"Lord Varick," she said, once their search brought them near enough to hear each other, "Were you born a vampire, or were you…*made* one?"

Silence followed for a moment. "Vempar," he corrected. "I am not of the undead. I'm simply another race of the Altered."

"Oh…" Rosen moved over to a patch of moss-covered ground.

"I suppose the *Nachzehrer* legend came from humans' fear of us. Why do you hate vampire creatures so much?" he continued.

"Hate? I don't—"

He gave her a look. The silver of his eyes both beautiful and unsettling.

"Fine. It makes me uncomfortable. My mother died, and the thought of her becoming a living corpse horrifies me. I know it could never happen, but the fact that people would believe such a thing possible is upsetting." She turned her head away, pretending to analyze moss.

"I am sorry the myths have caused you pain. Losing someone close to you is serious." Something in Varick's tone made her turn back—not just the tone of sympathy but understanding. As if he'd lost someone, too. She thought back to the painting of the Disteldorn family, and the once smiling boy.

She wanted to ask what had happened to his parents, the elegant couple, but instead she asked, "Do vempars drink blood?"

Varick made a face of disgust. "No, gross. We absorb the life-energy of others, instead. Much more clean."

"Ah…that sounds worse."

"Does it? It's quite harmless in small amounts, or so I'm told. I have vials of life-energy transported to me, so I've never actually had to…you know, get it for myself."

Varick pressed his cheek against the trunk of a beech tree on a patch of fluffy moss. When she looked at him funny, he flushed pink. "What? Moss is soft. I like the way it feels."

Rosen shrugged her shoulders. "I didn't say anything." Her mouth tweaked, trying not to grin.

He frowned at her.

Rosen weaved her way past two other beech trees, when her feet suddenly plummeted beneath her and she fell with a whoosh of leaves. She cried out, landing inside a hidden pit of mud.

Varick rushed over to the edge. When he saw her, his mouth opened and he burst out laughing. Rosen sat where she'd landed, blinking up at the pit's rim.

So, he was capable of laughter at her expense, was he?

She jumped to her feet and with her one hand grabbed the hem of Varick's cape, yanking hard so that he lost his balance and fell in.

With a yelp, he splashed into the mud. And when he lifted his head, half his face was caked in brown.

Rosen snorted and laughed, clutching her stomach.

Varick pouted and threw a handful of mud at her. She ducked to the side, scooped up mud and threw it at his chest, covering his pristine cravat. She giggled at the expression of utter shock on his face.

He flung another scoop of mud at her, caking her hair. His mouth lifted as he tried yet failed to hide a grin.

He finally did laugh when she pelted him with volley after volley in retaliation, fast for a single-handed person.

Finally, they tired out, and Rosen let her seat sink in the

mud as she sat, panting.

Varick smoothed his mud-thick hair back with a hand, then bent to pick her up in his arms.

"What—?" she started.

"Trust me," he said. She didn't completely, but let him carry her. He bent his legs, and in one jump he vaulted out of the pit and onto firm forest floor. He let Rosen down, her face wide-eyed.

He retrieved their baskets of mushrooms. "I suppose we found enough for today," he said.

They came back to the castle, a muddy mess, and nearly scared Butler Sterbetod to death. The butler wheezed worse than usual and hurried with an old man's speed from the castle door. "Licht, Schatten! A little…help!"

The nymiads arrived, and their expressions couldn't be put into words.

"Master," Licht said once he recovered. "Did you forget that the showers aren't working?"

Varick's small grin melted and became something like horror.

"I'm kidding, we fixed it already." Licht waved his palms.

Varick's horror became a tight-lipped glare.

Fee-ee-ee! laughed the red thistle pixit, watching them from behind a stone column.

As Varick and Rosen made their way towards the nearest washing station, Schatten hovered about in a panic. "Don't touch that! And keep away from the rugs—those are priceless! Oh my gracious, you're spreading mud *everywhere!*"

Mrs. Moos wrapped them each in towels and led them to separate shower rooms.

VARICK'S HAIR HAD FINALLY FINISHED drying before the fireplace. He brushed it back, keeping wavy strands out of his eyes, and rose from an upholstered chair.

Where had Rosenrot gone off to? For some reason sitting alone in a room made him feel bored. He used to be perfectly fine by himself, studying through books about woodlands and weather and astronomy. But now he just couldn't sit still.

He peeked inside the drawing room—Rosenrot wasn't there.

He wandered down the hallway of living quarters and peeked into another room—Rosenrot wasn't in her room, either.

Blast it, where was the girl?

His ears caught a rubbing noise, a circular motion, coming from up ahead. He stepped quietly toward the opposite end of the hallway, past a rail and curving staircase. The door to his parents' quarters was open and sunlight spilled onto the floor. He hesitated, then peeked inside.

The drapes had been thrust aside, and there Rosenrot stood, scrubbing away at the windows with her single hand.

His first instinct was to shout that she stop—he never allowed anyone in this room, let alone things in it be touched. But she was working diligently, and already had one window sparkling clean, bringing life into the lifeless space. Mother would never have let the place get so dusty. She always liked the sunlight sparkling through.

The green lacy dress Rosenrot wore had once been his mother's, when she was young. It fit her beautifully, and the stump that was her elbow didn't look as scary as the day when they first met. Actually, it looked rather pretty, sculpted, as if the Maker had wanted to try something different.

The girl must have spotted his reflection; she turned around and dipped her head. "I thought you might like to see this room the way it used to be, cleaned and lived in. If you want to preserve their memory, you can't let moths and whatnot eat away at it."

Varick blinked at her, then lowered his gaze. Her eyes were a chestnut shade, like the rich soil of a forest. Why hadn't he noticed that before?

"Ah...yes," he said. "But it's not like I asked you to do this. If you're bored, I can find other things—"

"Bored?" She frowned over her shoulder. "If I needed to cure boredom, I can think of a hundred better things to do! I'm just tidying up this room because it's special to you, and it'll decay if no one else does."

Something inside Varick's chest twitched in pain. He resisted the urge to cover it with a hand. Why would she do this?

"I don't understand," he finally said. "I haven't done anything for you, except purchase your labor. Why should you care about what's special to someone else?"

Rosenrot looked at him, tilting her head as if he were a puzzle. "You really have grown up isolated," she said. "Hasn't anyone ever done something for you simply because they care about you? Surely Licht and Mrs. Moos have."

Varick jerked his head to the side. "They're servants. They don't do anything because they care."

The girl's lips pursed in thought. "Or maybe you just don't pay attention well enough. I can tell they care about you."

Varick shrugged uncomfortably. "How would you know? Has anyone ever cared about you?"

Rosenrot stopped her work, dropping the rag into a bucket and carrying it out the door past him.

He realized it was the wrong thing to say after he'd say it.

She marched stiffly down the hallway, and he followed after.

"I didn't…I didn't mean it quite like that," he tried to say. But what *was* the right thing to say? What was he supposed to do? Ah, this was why he didn't want to be around people! They were too complicated to figure out. One wrong word, or a certain tone of voice, could ruin everything.

Rosenrot whirled around on him, and he lurched to a halt not to bump into her. "For your information, no. No one has ever cared about me. Not even my only family member, who ran away leaving me with all his debt to pay off. But I've seen other families, and friends, and the way they support one another and celebrate the holidays together. I know what it should be like to have someone to care for, and who in turn cares for me…even if I'll never have that, myself." A wetness glittered in her soft chestnut eyes, and he realized it must be tears.

Varick hung his head and wrung his hands together. "I didn't mean to hurt you. I'm not very good at communicating with others."

Rosenrot sniffled.

"I've just never had anyone do something nice for me, unless I ordered them to," he confessed.

She shook her head. "I can't even begin to imagine ordering people around." She sighed. "But I guess if no one's ever taught you how to behave, how are you supposed to know anything? Fine, how about I become your very first friend, then? I'll try and teach you how to behave proper."

She dropped the bucket and held out her hand. Varick stared at it, then tentatively clasped his hand with hers. Her skin felt warm. A tingly sensation ran through him, the comfort of touching someone, and then that sharp twinge of pain in his chest came again.

Her cheeks blushed slightly, and he wondered if his face was doing the same.

"I have a human friend. I never would have imagined that happening," he half-laughed quietly.

"Nor I imagine ending up in a creepy castle with a vamp— erm, vempar friend," she said.

Varick smirked.

A loud clang echoed up from the first floor.

"Master…Varick!" called an elderly voice. Butler Sterbetod hobbled and wobbled halfway up the staircase as they came around the bend. "Oh, there…you are. The…Lord Kalt is…here to see you," he said in between wheezes.

"Lord Kalt?" Rosenrot looked as if she'd been struck by lightning.

Varick wondered at her odd reaction. "Yes, he visits once a month or so."

"But why?" She shuddered as if chilled.

"He brings me life-energy supplies—I wouldn't survive without them." Varick trotted down the stairs without waiting.

Butler Sterbetod opened the front doors, wrist joints cracking, and Lord Kalt entered. He was followed by a strange, tall servant pushing a cart full of boxes.

"Lord Kalt, welcome." Varick greeted. Rosen hung back near the staircase, half hidden. The man's dark beard came down to such a sharp point, it was a wonder it didn't cut anything.

Kalt took off his slick gloves and gray wool coat, tossing them to Sterbetod, who nearly toppled over catching it all.

"How are things in the town?"

"Much the same. Full of people complaining about one thing or another," replied Kalt. The crescent moons embroidered on his robes shimmered in the entry's lamplight. "Anything new to report up here in the mountains?"

"No, it's as quiet as ever," said Varick.

The tall servant wheeled the cart off to the side, his skin slick porcelain. Rosen moved to better hide, and her elbow bumped a vase behind her. She whipped around and caught it, but the noise had still alerted her presence.

"Who is that?" Kalt demanded, his gaze hard as stone on Rosen, as she straightened and curtsied.

"A hired servant," Varick said nonchalantly. "The castle needed more cleaning."

Kalt's gaze on her lingered, suspicious. "You could have told me, and I would have lent you workers," his tone almost berated. "You didn't have to force yourself to hire a human."

Varick waved the matter away with a hand. "It's fine. But I'm glad you came today—my supplies were running low."

He led the way, and he and Lord Kalt vanished into a side hall and through into one of the parlor rooms, the fireplace inside already lit and wafting heat.

Rosen edged past the strange porcelain-like servant and stopped beside the open door to listen. The emotionless servant merely glanced her way.

"Lord Kalt, I'm eternally grateful for all that you've done for me," Varick was saying. "But I am curious, what do you use my blood for?"

Rosen risked a peek inside the room.

Varick sat on a chair opposite Kalt, a needle in the vein of his arm drawing blood through a string of tubing and flowing into a metallic cylinder.

"Haven't I told you?" Kalt said, a touch impatient, like a master to a young pupil. "Vempar blood contains extraordinary healing capabilities. I donate to shelters for the Altered, to those suffering from human-inflicted injuries or illness. It is a noble cause."

Varick nodded, believing his word. "Perhaps I should visit the shelters, or have some of them move to the castle—there's plenty of room here."

"No, it would only frighten them," Kalt said firmly. "Humans are not the only ones who fear vempars; even many Altered do."

Varick closed his mouth and looked down at the floor.

The cylinder clicked, and Kalt removed the needle and pressed a button that wound up the tubing.

"Don't be troubled. You're doing plenty of good by simply

being here in this castle."

They moved towards the door, and Rosen scurried into a different room, out of sight. "I will see you next month, Varick. Contact me if any…problems arise with your new servant."

Rosen swallowed on the other side of the wall. Fee the pixit was there, floating around her curiously.

She listened to the sounds as Varick escorted the lord outside. She waited until she was sure the man had gone before coming out.

"You have some sort of deal with Lord Kalt?" asked Rosen, once Varick came back indoors.

Varick hunched his shoulders defensively. "He saved my life once. I wouldn't call it a deal, but me simply repaying my debt to him."

"Isn't he human?" she asked carefully.

His brow pinched. "No! Yes. I mean, he's human but with strange powers. Like…like a mage, almost, though he said that wasn't exactly the proper title. But either way, he's nothing like the heartless humans in Freudendorf."

He flinched after he said it, some of his defensive posture slumping. "I don't mean you. Just…the others."

Rosen inhaled, bracing herself. "But the town is falling apart under Kalt. There's something cold and treacherous about him. Varick, you could restore the town, couldn't you? You could reopen the salt mines in these mountains. People are too afraid to come near your castle and the mines, now, but that would change if you invited them up here and showed them there's nothing to be afraid of."

"I don't want humans around here, and I don't care about the town. You…don't understand."

Varick assumed an even heavier defensive posture, chin high.

"Help me understand." Rosen drew near and touched his arm. He seemed surprised by the gesture. "What did the town do to you?"

His mouth opened and closed repeatedly. Then he gently brushed her hand off and headed for the staircase. "Ask Licht. Let him tell you the story," he said, unable to look back at her.

9

NINE-YEAR-OLD VARICK SKIPPED about the forest, collecting in his palms an assortment of colorful items. Once finished, he trotted back into the castle grounds, through the meandering gardens, to where Mother sat reading.

Her black curls trailed down her back like thick ribbons of night.

"Oh my, what have you brought me today?" she said when he trotted up to her.

He held out his hands for her to see.

"Blue and purple mushrooms, how lovely," she said. "And white wildflowers; they smell so fragrant! And is this moss? What a splendid bouquet you've made."

"It's for you, Mama!" He hopped up and down.

She took the wild assortment. "My, thank you." She smiled warmly. "Dinner is almost ready, dear. And your papa just arrived home. Let's go inside and see him, hm?"

She took his hand in hers. "Papa's back!" he cheered.

The dining room, when they entered, was all decorated for the Autumn Festival, and Varick's eyes gleamed with pure delight. Pumpkins and colorful squashes lined the mantles and made table centerpieces. Strings of colorful leaves and acorns hung from the arched ceiling and wrapped around decorative columns ringing the room.

"What do you think of our work, young Master?" asked Licht, one of the many nymiads working and living in the castle.

"It's beautiful!" Varick exclaimed.

Schatten nodded. "Good. It would be a shame if no one else appreciated the décor. Do you know how long it took to string all those acorns and leaves? They kept breaking apart; it was a nightmare, I tell you."

"You whine too much, Schatten," said another nymiad, his sister, to which all the others laughed.

"Varick, I brought you your favorite." His father appeared around a corner, traveling cape still on, and a tin box in his arm. His silver eyes smiled.

"Papa!" Varick ran to him, hugging his middle.

Papa laughed and tousled his hair. Varick snatched the box and eagerly opened it. The scent of pumpkin spice filled his nostrils when he did. "Pumpkin crumpets!" His feet danced in place with glee, and he popped a crumpet into his mouth.

"Now dear, eat dinner first," said Mama.

"Oh let him be a kid. It only lasts for so long," said Grandmamma, who lived in the castle with them. She shuffled over and crouched to Varick. "How about we go carve faces into those pumpkins I bought, afterwards?"

"Yes, yes!" Varick bounced on his heels.

Such a happy day that was. Everything festive and perfect, his family all around him, the castle merry and bright.

He'd carved pumpkins with Grandmamma on the floor, making a mess, while the nymiads laughed and egged him on to carve silly faces. And the pumpkin desserts after dinner were the best he'd ever had.

He ate while Papa told them stories of his travels. He loved listening to his tales about distant cities and strange cultures. It fueled Varick's imagination.

"I want to see the outside world, Papa!"

Papa smiled and patted his head, tousling his thick hair. "When you're older, how about that? I'll show you all my favorite places."

Yes, a wonderful day it had been, Varick recalled. Who could ever have known that the following morning would change his bright world forever…?

Varick woke to the sound of shattering glass. It was followed by shouts.

He yanked his robe on quickly and ran into the hallway, towards the staircase to see what the commotion was.

Grandmamma met him at the top stair. "Varick, come here! We have to leave!" Panic trembled in her voice.

"What's going on?" Varick moved to see around her.

She tried to block him but he dashed to the balcony section and looked down onto the entry hall.

A nightmarish scene spread before him. People dressed in black were climbing in through broken windows—humans, fangless and with round ears. They carried guns and crossbows and torches.

Papa was in the fray, punching and kicking, using his vempar speed and strength to cut down the humans. But more and more kept pouring in, like a stream of insects.

A cluster of nymiads tried to fight back the tide, wielding an assortment of blades and fire.

"Grandmamma, take Varick and go!" Papa shouted, sparing only a glance to meet their gazes above.

It was then that Varick saw Mama: lying on the cold floor not far from where Papa was battling. Wooden stakes stuck out of her chest, a trail of blood fell from the corner of her mouth.

"Mama?" Varick called out.

She wasn't moving. "Mama!" he shouted urgently.

"Varick!" Grandmamma caught his arm and began dragging him away.

"Mama... Mama, Mama!" he screamed. "Papa!"

"We love you, Varick. Now follow your Grandmamma!" called Papa's voice.

Varick couldn't stop the sobs and tears that tore out of him, as Grandmamma pulled him firmly away from the staircase and back toward the opposite end of the hallway, where there was a servants' staircase. They hurried down, feet muffled under a worn carpet.

Varick barely noticed where they were going, until they were already running through the backyard gardens, leaves and twigs snapping underfoot. With so much autumn foliage, it was impossible to mask their noise, and soon Varick heard a human shout.

"They've found us!" Grandmamma whispered to herself, her hand gripping his arm shaking.

More human voices came, and blasts echoed from guns. Bullets plinked the bushes and ground around them. "Varick, run! You're young, you can get away faster than I can," she told him.

Varick whipped his head from side to side. "I'm not leaving you!"

Blood trickled from Grandmamma's mouth. "You have to…" she wheezed.

"No! Why are they doing this?"

"Humans hate us. They've always…hated us…"

Another volley of bullets whizzed past, and Grandmamma fell forward, hitting her knees then sinking onto her side. "Run…" she could barely say.

A burning pain lanced through Varick's chest suddenly, and he wasn't sure if it was emotion or injury, until his chest felt wet as a breeze rolled past. He looked down to find his shirt and robe stained red, right where his heart should be.

He wanted to cry or scream, but his body simply sunk forward and his head rested against dirt and dry leaves. He blinked, trying to stay awake, trying to understand why all of this was happening.

The humans in their dark clothes approached, and one drew out a blade, slashing it across Grandmamma's throat. Varick tried to make his limbs move, tried to fight back, but the blade soon came towards him, slashing downward.

Kchnk!

A flash of silver light blasted the blade out of the male human's hand. He appeared puzzled for a second, and then more flashes of silver streaked through the air—cutting down humans like a scythe. Varick kept his eyes open, watching, stunned.

A man in dark robes came into his vision, the flashes coming from him, or rather from his robe, silver crescent moons that sliced through the air like blades. Varick wasn't sure when it ended, but he suddenly saw the strange man kneeling before him, touching his chest.

"This wound will kill you," the man told him. "But I have something that can freeze the wound in place so that you will live. If that is what you want?"

Varick didn't know if his parents were still alive, but if they were, then he had to survive too. He nodded slightly.

The man pulled something out from his robes: a band of silver with a ruby in the shape of a rose, and clicked it around Varick's neck. "This mage artifact can keep you alive, but only under one condition: You must never fall in love. If you do, the spell will break and you will die."

Varick remembered the feel of life returning to his body as the artifact did its work. And he remembered racing towards the front of the castle, hurrying into the entry hall, only to find his parents both lay dead on the slick floor.

Deceased humans and nymiads also littered the space. Varick's stomach heaved, like it never had before.

Vempars could heal from most injuries, but they had limits. His parents' hearts had been torn out. And his own heart was missing a large piece, in more ways than one.

Varick came to know the man who had saved him as Lord Kalt, a user of magic—or whatever it was. He helped Varick bury his parents, and his magic worked to clean and fix the damage done. He promised to take over the ruling of the human town below, in place of his parents, and would make sure they never attacked or approached the castle again.

Not being able to love didn't seem like a difficult thing for Varick, then. There was no one left in his life to love. He kept the curse a secret, though, telling Licht and the others who'd survived that the artifact would merely make his appearance ugly if he ever loved someone.

He didn't want anyone to know the truth: that the wound to his heart would reappear and he would die.

Varick opened his eyes now, staring up at the canopy over his bed glittering with silver stars. Rosen wouldn't know the truth about the curse, just as Licht did not know.

It was better that way.

10

ROSEN SIPPED AT HER BOWL of hot pumpkin soup, seated across the dining table from Varick. She thought over what Licht had told her of the Disteldorn family tragedy, and how only Varick had survived—and that because of Kalt. But it wasn't enough to make her feel better about the mage. She felt the sensation of spiders crawling up her skin just thinking about him.

She watched as Varick tried to use a spoon more daintily. His thick black eyelashes contrasted heavily with the pale skin of his features. His behavior made more sense now, especially his revulsion of humans. Why would they do something so wicked, and to a family that had ruled over and cared for the town many generations? Perhaps they'd grown tired of their authority? A rich versus the poor type of thing? But…something about the whole situation just didn't sit right with her.

"There's still a little light outside," she said conversationally. "Would you show me where the mines are? I'm in the mood to go exploring."

Varick's brow furrowed. "Exploring in a mine? You do know it's only salt you'll find there—not diamonds."

"I'm not looking for diamonds but adventure." She made a face. "Friends should go on adventures together."

Varick took a sip of *apfelschorle*. "Fine, if you say so."

Rosen finished the *schnitzel* on her plate, which she noticed had been pre-cut into small pieces for her. Had it been Mrs. Moos's idea, or…?

She glanced up at Varick. He seemed to be busy avoiding eye contact.

Rosen put on a warmer dress and cloak, and followed Varick out into the darkening mountain forest. He held a lantern aloft, the glass burnt tinted from use.

The path they took climbed for several minutes, and he held his hand for her, helping her over a couple of boulders.

Insects still chirped in the night despite the cold, and an owl was out hunting, its soft hoot carrying through the autumn canopy.

The trees eventually parted before a small clearing, a cave yawning there into the mountainside. "This connects to the salt mines. It's faster," Varick told her.

He led the way inside. A gust of air shoved Rosen's hair back as she entered, and a cool dampness brushed along her skin.

The pool of lantern light made veins of rock shimmer in the curved walls as they followed the tunnel downward into the earth. Chirps alerted her to bats: high on the ceiling of the cave they crossed. Rocks took on strange, sharp shapes around them, and after meandering through the length of stalactites and stalagmites, a set of stairs chiseled into the cave floor led them down and to the side of a crossing tunnel.

"And these are the mine tunnels," Varick announced, his voice bouncing back along the walls. It was much colder and damp here. She could almost taste the salt in the air.

"Which way?" She looked about.

He motioned left.

Thick wood shafts ran along the walls and ceiling at intervals here, maintaining the tunnel's structure and stability. When a space opened suddenly before them, the floor ended at an edge and plunged down into darkness.

As she listened, she could hear the echo of tapping and hammering work being done. "Aren't these mines abandoned?" She scrunched her brow at Varick.

"As far as I knew," he replied offhandedly.

Who could be down there mining salt? It wasn't anyone from Freudendorf, that much was certain.

Rosen searched about. "There aren't any stairs… How are we supposed to get down there?"

Varick simply pointed at a wooden slide.

"Oh no…no no no. I'm not doing that." She shook her head vigorously.

"Then I guess this will remain a mystery. Let's go back; my hair is starting to frizz." He turned.

She grabbed his elbow, and he stumbled. "I have to know who's down there. I can't leave a mystery that's staring me in the face unsolved."

He smirked and took a seat on the slide. He patted the spot in front of him. "With our combined weight, we should be fine. Miners use slides like these all the time."

Rosen regarded the spot. He waited.

She swallowed her nerves and gingerly sat in front. Her back leaned against his chest, and he wrapped his arms around her. Her cheeks heated.

"Ready?"

But before she could answer, he pushed them forward and the world tilted down in a burst of speed.

Air whipped past, ripping her breath away.

How were they going to stop?

As soon as she began panicking, the drop leveled out; but their momentum kept them going, until she was sure they'd fly off the end of the slide and into an endless abyss.

Varick's heels dug down, and their speed slowed. Somehow they gradually came to a halt.

Varick hopped off as if it had been fun, but Rosen staggered and took his offered hand.

Faint lights appeared in the distance, following along branching tunnels of salt rock. Rosen moved carefully, taking the right-hand tunnel. Varick peered over her shoulder.

The chamber beyond echoed of metal chipping salt. The workers were tall, their skin lumpy and droopy, like layers of batter—no, they looked made of clay.

They were golems.

Rosen started, remembering a piece of folklore about golems: creatures created from dark magic, having no life, no will, but to follow their master's commands. Someone had created them to mine the salt, stealing it away from Freudendorf. Was that why rumors had spread that these mines were cursed and forbidden? To keep people from coming here and discovering this theft?

"Strange…" Varick whispered. His breath tickled her neck.

One golem finished loading a wheelbarrow and started pushing it towards the chamber's opposite tunnel.

"I'm following!" Rosen whispered. She crept along the chamber wall on hand and knees, keeping the wheelbarrow in sight—following into the tunnel and praying no passing golem would look down and spot her.

Two golems passed by the wheelbarrow golem, coming from the opposite way.

She crouched and froze still. They lumbered past in a lurching gait, empty eyes made of hard clay staring straight ahead, focused on the task at hand. Once they were past, she hurried on.

It was a long walk before the tunnel opened to the night sky, leading out onto a space of gravel jutting out the side of the mountains.

She crouched at the entrance, watching as the golem unloaded large cubes of orange-tinted salt into a hefty sack.

"This entrance looks newer," Varick commented behind her.

The golem lifted its head, knobby clay ears twitching.

She wanted to smack Varick. But the creature continued and heaved the full sack of salt onto its back and began lumbering down an obscure path, down through the sloping forest.

She hurried after. The path rounded boulders and made steep declines. Varick's grip kept her from losing her balance, and tree trunks made for good handholds. A steady north wind helped mask their noise.

The path reached the valley floor and edged around the outskirts of the town. Rosen suddenly had a hunch as to where the golem was headed. And it was confirmed when they rounded a bend and came within view of a mansion on top a hill, just outside Freudendorf. A mansion with stately columns, contrasting with the friendly gingerbread half-timbered houses beyond.

"That's where Lord Kalt lives," she informed Varick. His eyebrows shot up, though he didn't seem much concerned.

The little path cut around to the back of the hill, to an obscure area that anyone would have easily overlooked. But she followed the golem with her eyes through the brush and to a concealed door that swung open for the golem as it carried the sack of salt inside.

Rosen hurried to catch the door before it closed, and found there was no handle. But the door detected her movement and swung open again.

"Some sort of trigger spell?" she wondered.

Inside was a storage chamber, and the golem tossed the sack onto a pile before lumbering back towards the exit. Rosen and Varick slipped behind a stack of crates in the chamber as the golem's lumpy face drifted past.

The door closed on its own, and Rosen dashed forward to investigate, stealing Varick's lantern and relighting it.

The salt sacks made one pile, while crates of salt sacks made another—the crates had Lord Kalt's crescent moon symbol, like a trademark, as if he were selling the crates somewhere...

"Oh my word, Varick. He's selling the salt to foreigners! Making a profit off what should belong to the town!" She fumed.

"And the rest of the salt?" Varick fiddled with a loose thread on a sack.

She thought. "It looks like he's keeping it, using it for himself? Though I can't imagine what he would use so much salt for."

Varick shrugged. "I don't care what he does with the salt. The town deserves what's happening to it." He headed back for the door. "I'm leaving. Your little mystery is solved."

"Are you being haughty with me? Friends don't treat

friends rudely," she snapped.

He halted in his steps, heaved a sigh. "I wasn't trying to—Fine. I'll wait right here for you." He dusted a crate off before sitting.

Giving a nod, Rosen held the lantern light out to every corner, every nook of the chamber. She detected a thin line and thought it must be another concealed door. But when she waved and moved around, nothing happened.

"Hey, Varick, come over here and pull this door open."

He grumbled, came, and squinted at the thin gap. He gave her a look. "How is this a door?"

"It is! Trust me," she insisted.

He frowned but gripped the tips of his fingers along the line, and pulled. The door material shuddered slightly but stayed put.

Grimacing more, Varick dug his fingernails in and braced both feet against the dirt floor. He pulled and tugged, putting his vempar strength into it.

Finally, the door groaned open.

"I'm guessing Kalt has a special way only he can open this," she murmured. "Thanks, Varick!"

He shrugged with a little proud smile, dusting off his hands.

The space inside was small and littered with shelves and books. She crept in. The most noticeable thing present was a leather book that sat open on a narrow table.

Rosen tiptoed over.

Strange symbols were illustrated on the pages. The top right page was titled *Memory Shift*. And a series of instructions and ingredients followed.

She scanned over a snippet of the page illustrating star shapes, which needed to be drawn in a circle around the intended subject. A side note read that the spell, once cast, must be renewed monthly on a regular basis.

This was a book on magic—or something like it. But Varick didn't seem to think Kalt was a mage. That left only one other option: an ordinary human who wanted to wield the power of mages but by darker means, in other words, a warlock.

"Someone's coming!" Varick called out, just above a whisper.

Rosen jumped in her shoes with alarm. Her hand was tempted to take the book, or at least the page, to examine further, but then Kalt would know someone had been snooping around his secret lair.

With a frustrated grunt, she hurried out to Varick. He pushed the secret door closed, as she blew out the lantern, and together they slipped out the chamber in the hill and into the underbrush along the path. They made it just before a group of five golems lumbered past with sacks.

Varick led the way through the woods, heading back towards the western mountain foothills now that their investigation was at an end.

"So, Lord Kalt's a warlock. That must be why he creeps me out so much," she said, while she tried not to stub her toes on rocks poking out of leaf-covered forest floor. "*Memory Shift*; why was he reading that spell? It gives me a bad feeling. What if he's already used that spell on someone?"

Varick shrugged, pushing aside limbs and underbrush for them as she followed close at his back. "I don't know much about mages or warlocks, but Lord Kalt is the reason I'm still alive. Perhaps he studies spells for the same reason any researcher studies books on mushrooms and astronomy and whatever else. Studying a spell doesn't mean he's gone and used it."

Rosen cocked her head. That was true, but she just didn't like the feeling her gut was giving her.

"My feet ache…" she mumbled. Her legs weren't used to hiking uphill this much.

Varick turned around and in one swift movement swept Rosen off her feet and into his arms. He continued up the forest's incline as if it were a steady stroll, not breaking a sweat.

She felt her face redden, her heartbeat race. "Thanks…" she murmured. Her arm looped around his neck for support, and his face seemed so close. He didn't glance at her, or maybe tried not to. It wasn't easy to tell in the moonlight if his cheeks were flushed.

When they reached the high foothill and the castle gate, he set her down. Butler Sterbetod came wheezing, opening the gate and following them in. "Lord Varick…we were so…worried for you both…vanishing off…the way you did!" he tried to exclaim, though it was more the sound of a hissing balloon.

"Oh, sorry." Varick looked almost bashful. "I didn't think we'd be out long. It was just an excursion around the mines."

"You'll hear an…earful from Licht…that's certain!"

Which, he did. Though, much to Licht's vexation, Varick hardly listened and went and took a luxurious bath.

Later that night, as Rosen slipped warm socks over her feet before tucking into bed, her thoughts kept going back to the page in the spell book and all of the town's salt profits being snatched away.

The fireplace crackled warmly, its light meeting that of the moon across the rug.

But what should she do? How could she expose what Kalt was doing to the town?

And whose memory was he planning on tampering with?

DUKE GASTO GATHERED EVERY OUNCE of courage in his spirit he could muster, and he marched up to the looming iron gate of the gothic castle.

The two guards standing armed behind him gave small comfort, their metal plates shaking.

Frozen morning dew crunched under his boots. Between two curled bars, a frozen spiderweb shimmered. Gasto looked about, then reached to yank the right half gate open.

"Excuse me, sir…" someone wheezed.

A gray-green man with wild strands of ancient hair appeared, as if out of nowhere.

Gasto bounded backwards with a surprised yelp.

Was this a zombie or a man?

"What is it…you want…sir?" the zombie-man finished asking.

Gasto stood blinking for a moment, then shook his head to clear it. "I—I came here to find the lovely Miss Rosenrot. There's been a mistake, you see. I'm the one who was supposed to buy her labor. I'll be more than glad to buy her off this…Lord Varick's hands."

He waited, and the zombie tilted his head with a creak then slowly turned his back. "In that case…I shall inform Lord Varick…of your intentions…"

Gasto watched through the decorative gate bars as the old man made his way down the ramshackle path to the castle. He tapped his foot and grumbled at the sky impatiently.

A long while later, a form in a dark cape came striding out the castle. Gasto readied himself, but in the blink of an eye the form appeared before him, on his side of the gate.

Gasto jumped back, hand instinctively reaching for his sword.

"Duke Pasto," said the man, not much older than himself, but taller and built more lean, dressed in the wealthy suit of a lord, hair in neat layered waves. His eyes glowed like molten silver.

"It's Gasto," he corrected meekly.

"Well, that's even worse," said Varick. "Duke Gasto, I hear you've come to take away my servant, who I hired." His tone sounded accusing. "What gives you such a right?"

Gasto had to grab onto his courage before it melted away. There were rumors about this castle, and about the things who lived here. Was this Varick even human?

"I—I would pay you back whatever you ask for her," said Gasto. "I and Rosenrot have known each other for years, you see. She'd be much more comfortable working for me, someone she knows."

A strange fire lit in Lord Varick's eyes.

"Will you ask her? If it's workers you need, I have plenty of servants I could lend you—"

In a flash of movement both of Gasto's guards fell on their backs, and Varick reappeared in front of him, hands holding both their and Gasto's swords.

Gasto looked to his belt in a panic, finding it empty.

"Miss Rosenrot belongs with me. I don't care what your past is, her future now is here." Varick dropped the swords; they clattered on the old pavestones loudly. "Now leave. Before the *Nachzehrer* decides to make a meal of you all." His fangs flashed in the early dawn light.

Gasto nearly shrieked, and stumbled backwards into his two guards, who scrambled upright.

"If—if I find anything's happened to Rosenrot, I'll make you pay!" Gasto shouted before hurrying away back down the sloping path towards town, not even bothering to retrieve his sword.

Rosenrot passed by the entry hall as Varick closed the door behind him. "You were outside just now?" she asked.

Varick combed back his hair with a hand. "Dealing with a pest problem," he replied.

She wondered at that but continued on. "The Autumn Festival is tonight," she said, tapping the toe of her right shoe against the floor. "There will be singing and dancing and all the food you can imagine," she said wistfully. "I know you don't like humans, but…it might be fun to go. We can wear leaf masks so no one will recognize us." She met his gaze, waiting, pleading.

Varick shuffled uncomfortably, pale cheeks pinking.

"I suppose, if it means that much to you, and if we're disguised…"

Rosenrot bounced on her heels. "Yes! This will be so much fun! I need to go find a *dirndl* to wear. And you need a *bundhosen*."

Varick's eyebrows soared. "Me, dress like a weird peasant?"

"It isn't weird, it's traditional mountain folk clothing."

He made a revolted expression.

"Come on, you'll blend in better," she sing-songed.

He took a wary step back from her sudden cheerfulness.

Later that evening, Varick found himself wearing a black leather *bundhosen* Licht had found, the overalls ending at the knees while thick stockings covered the rest of his legs. The straps were annoying over his white dress shirt. Red and orange leaves were pinned all about his person, as if he'd fallen into a leaf pile, and a mask made of brown ferns and red bush leaves fit above his nose, hiding the top half of his face.

He felt like a fool.

"And now, presenting Miss Rosenrot!" announced Licht as he led Rosen down the stairs.

Varick's breath caught. Her *dirndl* dress was gold and white, embroidered with golden leaves. Some real leaves were pinned about her, as they were on Varick, and the mask around her eyes was golden maple and birch leaves. Like an autumn fairy out of folklore, she looked stunning.

A lance of pain pricked his heart, and he swallowed, trying to ignore it. He held his arm out for her to take, then realized it was the wrong arm.

She lifted what was left of her left arm anyway and pressed it against his inner elbow. How she managed to move and live so normally, making him forget about her disability entirely, was beyond him.

Together they stepped out into the cool evening, to a waiting black-and-gold carriage pulled by a large black horse, a gleaming horn growing from its head. Rosenrot stood marveling at the beast for a moment before stepping inside.

Freudendorf Town was alight with merry lanterns and lampposts and bracketed torches as they drew near. They parked the carriage in the shadows at the edge of the buildings, and Rosenrot led him towards the town's center square. On every side were vendors and tables and carts, making and selling crafts.

Women wove fine straw into ornaments: making little angels and snowflakes. One cart was layered and strung full of hand-painted eggshells. Varick stopped to wonder at them, touching an egg painted in pumpkins, the one beside it painted to resemble fairies.

People everywhere were dressed in traditional clothing, fancy *dirndls* and *bundhosen*. He didn't feel quite as foolish anymore. There were other people wearing leaf masks too, mostly the young adults and children.

Several kids dashed past Varick's legs and into the throng of citizens. He tried to keep calm, surrounded by so many people, so many humans.

Aromas filled the streets, and Rosenrot paused at some of the stalls. Potatoes and trout were roasting at one, and a man was busy making smoked ham and sausages at another. Fresh apples and every kind of apple dessert was on display from the recent harvest.

An old woman handed him a sample cup of drink. He took a careful sip then cringed at the strong *schnapps*. "*Ahem*, no thank you," he coughed.

Rosenrot gathered a bag of cheeses seasoned with herbs, and sausages. They sat on an empty portion of a bench to eat, while in the square's center before them people danced around a bonfire, *dirndls* swaying. Varick held the food for her.

Creamy herbed cheese melted in his mouth, mingling perfectly with the salty sausage. For dessert, he found *apfelstrudel*, heavy with sugar and cinnamon. He pulled apart chunks and plopped them into Rosenrot's mouth. She laughed, chewing.

"Let's dance!" Rosenrot hopped to her feet after they'd finished.

He stood, unsure, and she took his hand, pulling him forward into the dancing circle.

They held onto each other's shoulders, spinning round in hop-skip steps, making their way around the bonfire with the other couples.

He tried not to step on her toes. He felt like a clumsy horse.

"I haven't danced much before," he admitted to her.

She laughed. "As long as you hop with the rhythm, no one will ever know."

The firelight played along her golden leaf mask and short lavender hair, making her glow.

Merriment filled the air, almost overwhelming his senses, and the closeness of her as they danced sent his pulse pounding. A warm feeling wrapped his chest, and he began to laugh with her, spinning round and round.

Rosenrot was a wonderful friend, more than he could ever ask for. He held her close, never wanting to let go, never wanting to lose this feeling. If only he could caress her face and—

A sharp pain stabbed his chest, and his steps faltered.

"Varick?" Rosenrot looked up in concern.

She guided him out of the dancing throng and paused at a stand selling crusty cheese bread.

Varick clenched at his chest for a moment, then straightened, taking slow breaths. "It's just…too much excitement for one day, I suppose," he bluffed. But her eyebrows stayed concerned. "Are there any pumpkin desserts? Pumpkin always calms my nerves," he added to distract her.

"Mm, I'll go see," she said.

When she left, Varick flicked out a mirror and angled it to the necklace: another of the ruby petals had lost their life glow.

He breathed through his nose, calming his rapid pulse. If the glow in each ruby petal died out… But how could he control his feelings? Did he even want to anymore?

Lord Kalt watched from the opposite end of the bonfire as Rosenrot returned to Varick with slices of pumpkin pie. He adjusted his black leaf mask and turned aside.

He had seen it all—the way Varick had reacted.

The girl was a threat that would have to be taken care of. She could not be allowed to become Varick's downfall.

Varick stumbled under the weight of a pile of gourds and pumpkins as he carried them up to the castle doors. Rosenrot had insisted on buying them, and she now waved for him to hurry in.

"I don't see what you're so excited about. I've gone and

sullied my *dirndl* carrying this." He pouted.

But her good mood didn't falter, and she helped set the lot of produce onto the floor inside.

Weary, he slouched onto a sofa in the sitting room and watched as she darted about from the entry hall to the dining room and back, carrying items.

After a while observing, he pushed himself to his feet. "Should I...help?" he asked, not having a clue what it was he was offering to help with. She just kept dashing about so much that it made him feel restless.

"Almost finished," she said.

Varick cocked an eyebrow. "Finished with what?" he asked, following her into the dining room.

Rosenrot placed a handful of maple leaves on a table and twirled to face him, the fabric of her gold and white dress turning with her. She spread her arms wide, "With this! You can't celebrate the Autumn Festival without a festive house."

Varick stared about the dining room. Colorful centerpieces decorated the mantles and the long dining table: gourds of autumn greens, yellows, and oranges forming fantastical shapes between rings of bright leaves.

A memory flashed back of that day long ago: he and his family celebrating the festival in this room, the castle filled with color and life and cheer...

"Do you not like it?" Rosenrot said when he didn't speak.

"Oh." He shook himself back to the present. "It's beautiful. The most beautiful this place has looked in a long time." He meant it, in more ways than one, watching the firelight play on the gold leaves about her dress.

She smiled. "Good. I figured you would."

She covered a yawn and went over to plop down on the settee before the fireplace. "I'm too tired to go upstairs and change..." she mumbled.

Varick smirked. "Should I read you a bedtime story, then?" He lifted a book off the end table near the crackling fire and sat beside her, flipping through pages. "Ah, here we are. Ever read *The Seven Ravens*?"

She shook her head sleepily.

He began to read the old fairy tale aloud.

He was only several paragraphs in when something bumped his shoulder.

Varick glanced to the side. There, Rosenrot's head rested against his shoulder.

He felt his features flush bright pink. He almost pulled back in surprise then realized she had dozed off.

Rosenrot's face was peaceful, eyes fluttering beneath her lids in some unknown dream. A strand of lavender fell near to her nose.

He reached and with a finger brushed it back. But his hand lingered, lightly touching her cheek.

He wasn't alone anymore. The absence his dear family had left behind was slowly being filled again. And he felt...happy. He'd almost forgotten what that even felt like.

Another spike of pain made him clutch his chest. He waited for it to pass.

When it did, he let his chin rest lightly against the top of Rosenrot's head and drifted into sleep.

12

GASTO STOMPED DOWN A WINDING street, hands shoved in pockets, lips muttering to himself. How dare that creature Varick keep his dear Rosenrot locked up in that creepy castle, with creepy zombie servants!

Was she safe? What if that monster grew hungry and saw her as a snack? What if every night she was crying herself to sleep in fear?

He had to do something. He had to!

But what? Storm the castle? That was risky when he didn't know what sort of unnatural creatures he might have to face.

A hammering noise drew his gaze: a young boy fixing a paper onto a wood post. He left to distribute more to the next post.

Gasto wandered over and had a look. The paper read *Wanted: Rosenrot Hartmann, for thievery to Lord Kalt.*

"No. No, no, this must be a mistake!" He cupped a hand over his mouth. "The punishment for such thievery can be death…!"

The street rocked beneath his feet.

His fair Rosenrot—he couldn't let her die like this.

"Oh what should I do?" he moaned. "If she stays with that beast, she'll be eaten. But if she comes back to town, she'll be executed! Oh woe is me."

Pssst!

Gasto heard a sound and looked about.

Pssst!

It came again, from the shadows between two half-timbered houses.

As Gasto squinted, a glowing purple smile, purple eyes and ears materialized and beckoned to him. "You want Rosenrot, yes?" the creature asked.

Scared out of his wits, Gasto still drew near at the sound of the girl's name.

"Y-you know of her?" he said.

The shadowy creature took form the closer he came, shadows weaving a suit and flowing hair. "I do. I am Schatten, and I work at the forbidden castle," it said.

The castle? It dawned on Gasto then. "You know my Rosenrot! Does this mean you can help me free her from that awful place?"

Schatten shrugged up his shadowy palms. "If you give me something in return."

"Anything. Just name it!"

Schatten's smile glowed and he pushed off the alley wall. "Then give me the deeds to your forested land, every foothill you own, and in return I will bring you the girl."

Gasto hesitated for a moment before nodding. "*Ja*, if you bring her. But I still have another problem to solve… Lord Kalt will execute Rosenrot if she comes into town."

"That is a simple matter." Schatten steepled his fingers together. "Kalt simply wants the girl out of his way. But if you can get her to marry you, and stay away from the castle, then I'm certain he will allow her to keep her life. Go and ask him. Meanwhile, I will lure Miss Rosenrot to you…"

The next day, Rosen pruned a few of the trees in the gardens, while Varick worked to clear leaves away. She blushed remembering how she'd woken up that morning, snuggled against Varick on the settee. He hadn't teased her about it though, like she thought he might, but seemed flustered and eager to start work on a project: hence cleaning the gardens.

She wiped her forehead with the back of her hand and went back indoors for a drink.

Filling a mug with water, she sipped.

"Oh, Miss Rosenrot!" Schatten entered the kitchens. He drew near, his voice hushed. "I was just looking for you. There's someone at the gate who wishes to speak to you."

Rosen eyed him. "Who?" she asked warily.

"He wouldn't give his name, but…he shares quite a resemblance to you. A relative, perhaps?"

Relative.

Rosen only knew of one relative, and she had a bone to pick with him!

"Dad's come crawling back, has he? Well, we'll just see about that." She shucked off her apron and marched out the main doors.

While crossing the front courtyard, Mrs. Moos waved to her, come back from picking apples at the abandoned orchard.

"Where're you off to, dearie?"

Rosen waved. "I'll be back soon, don't worry."

Schatten followed along behind her. She could feel the moss woman watching her back curiously.

Rosen marched to the gate and stepped through, onto the paved clearing, her hand on her hip.

She turned her head, but no one seemed to be there. Something rustled in the bushes up ahead, the same ones where she had hidden years back.

"I know it's you, Dad. You may as well come out and face me properly," she said, and marched forward.

As she reached the bushes, a man stepped free, flinging leaves out of his brown hair. She started in confusion. "Gasto?"

"Hi there." He waved.

Just when he did, a pair of arms pinned her hand to her side and covered her mouth. She tried to scream and kick free.

"Now, now, there's no need to fuss, my dear Rosenrot," he told her.

Her head felt dizzy. Something in the guard's hand that covered her mouth was affecting her. Her body tried to flail but grew limp, and the world around fell dark.

Varick lifted his head. The sun was dipping below the mountains, rimming their edges in sharp gold, and Rosenrot hadn't come back since noon. Maybe she'd gotten distracted with another project?

But as he circled the grounds, and wandered the castle hallways, she was nowhere to be found. "Licht, have you seen Rosenrot?" he asked as the fire nymiad carried a load of dirty rags downstairs.

"Miss Rosenrot? Why, no. I thought she was with you."

Varick frowned. He turned at the approach of Schatten, rounding on the shadowy figure. "And you? Have you seen Rosenrot?"

Schatten lifted his eyebrows in thought. "Ah, yes, I did see her."

"Where?" Varick demanded, struggling not to let his impatience show.

"Last I saw, she was heading down the path towards town."

"Town? She went into town without telling me? Without you bothering to say anything?"

"I assumed you knew, Master." Schatten feigned innocence. "You don't suppose she saw her chance at escape and took off? She is human, after all. She doesn't belong here."

Licht shushed him, then patted Varick's arm. "I'm sure the girl will be back soon. Maybe there was something urgent calling her today."

Varick pulled away. "Maybe…either that, or she got tired of me and left." He crossed his arms and hunched his shoulders.

"Now don't go getting broody and sulky, Master. You always jump to the worst conclusions," huffed Licht.

"Because the worst is usually true." Varick stormed up the stairs, slamming the drawing room door behind him.

Varick tried to relax in his comfortable, lush chair but couldn't, instead pacing back and forth before the window overlooking the front courtyard and the path leading through to the gate and the forest beyond.

A burning pain crept through his chest, making it hard to breathe. He glanced at one of the room's mirrors: five of the ruby rose's petals had darkened. There were only five more left—five left to keep him alive.

Rosenrot was gone, and he had doomed himself; he never should have let his heart grow feelings for the girl. Her intelligent smile. Her adventurous spirit. Her...

He wiped his damp eyes.

The sky was dimming slowly into twilight when a knock came and Mrs. Moos brought in a fresh batch of life-energy rich apple tarts. The sight of food made his stomach bitter for some reason.

"I don't understand what I did wrong," he finally said, before the moss woman left the door. She paused. "Rosenrot seemed...happy, I thought. Why would she suddenly up and leave? But then, I've never been able to read emotions well." He shrunk in on himself.

"Oh, the sweet human girl? I saw her earlier heading out the gate with Schatten," said Mrs. Moos.

Varick's head turned to her sharply. "With Schatten? He was with her?"

"I do believe so. At least, that's what my eyes did tell me. Is she all right?"

Varick's mind began to race.

Schatten had lied to him—a nymiad, who had served his family for years, had lied!

The shock made his pulse pound in his ears. What else had he lied about? Did Rosenrot really choose to leave, or...?

"Schatten!" Varick shouted, his voice carrying through the hallways and columns of the castle.

When no answer came, he stormed out of the room like a prowling lion. "Schatten, come here this instant!"

The only response was his echo.

Flickering flames announced Licht, hurrying along the balcony towards him. "Master, what's happened?" His foggy features held worry.

"Schatten has lied to me. He's done something with Rosenrot, and I must know what!"

"Lied? But…" Licht looked just as stunned as he'd felt earlier. "Are you sure, Master?"

"Find him!" He twirled on his thicker black cape and jumped off the balcony, dismissing the stairs and landing in the entry hall, feet thudding the marble floor. "I will find Rosenrot."

Down at the gate, Varick followed the path to the bushes as fog crept over the landscape. Her shoeprints were there—and mixed with others.

The only person he could think of who might be after her…it had to be that Duke Pasto. He could even smell a faint residue of cologne.

What role Schatten played in this, he would have to figure out later.

"You will pay a heavy price for this," he growled to the air, the pain in his chest now a continual burn.

13

ROSEN LIFTED HER HEAD, SQUINTING and blinking rapidly to clear the haze from her vision.

She lay on a sofa, and the wide window at her back showed the sun fading behind the mountain peaks. Before her a fireplace crackled, and seated there nervously in a plush chair was Gasto.

He leaped to his feet when he saw her wake.

"Rosenrot, careful not to sit up too quickly. Here, I brought you some coffee and cookies." He indicated the low marble table before her.

She rubbed at her forehead and shook herself awake, then peered at the coffee, tempted by the caffeine but wary.

"It's not drugged," he said as if reading her thoughts.

"And I didn't want to drug you earlier—really and truly. But there was no other way to get you here." His tone pleaded, yet as if his actions were justified, and he kneeled beside the table, reaching for her hand, which she quickly moved.

"Do tell me what you hoped to accomplish by bringing me here?" she replied tartly.

Gasto's eyes widened as if it were obvious. "Why, to save you from the fate of becoming *that* beast's next meal! I couldn't leave you in such a predicament, not my dear Rosenrot. I couldn't let you become soup—though, I'm sure you would have made the best soup ever, since you're so tenderly sweet."

She gave him a weird look, and he cleared his throat.

"You must have been terrified, being kidnapped by that beast and forced to serve him."

"The only one who's kidnapped me is *you*," she said flatly. Her head was spinning and she took a chance at the coffee, gulping it down.

"Perhaps now that things are settled, you can finally put this on." Gasto opened a case, revealing a sapphire ring to her. "I know we will make the most beautiful couple in Freudendorf!"

Couple? Ring?

"Are—are you asking me to marry you?" Rosen spluttered.

"I will make you the happiest woman in the world, I promise. No price will be too much! You can have whatever your exquisite heart desires." He moved to slip the ring on her finger, but she pulled her hand back, tucking it against her side.

"I'm sorry, Gasto, but I'm not in love with you. You deserve a girl who will adore you and your...wealthiness," she said.

"Love?" He flapped his hand at that. "Who needs love to be married? As long as we can get along, that's all that matters. Now here, put this on," he tried again.

Rosen scooted to the farthest end of the sofa.

Gasto sighed. "My parents were perfectly happy together, and they weren't in love. Can't you give us a chance?"

"Where are your parents? I've never seen them," she said, the fact suddenly striking her as odd.

"They're…traveling on business." Gasto tilted his head, as if unsure and trying to remember.

"What kind of business? Why would a wealthy family like yours move here, to such a remote town?"

Gasto seemed confused, his brow pinching together. "They…they…" He searched for an answer, finding nothing. He rubbed the sides of his head suddenly, as if fighting a bad headache. "I don't remember why… *Why* don't I remember why?"

Rosen's stomach clenched. Gasto couldn't remember because someone had affected his memory. Lord Kalt's memory spell.

"Gasto, is it true that many years ago a group of humans from town stormed the castle and killed the Disteldorn family?" she asked.

Gasto looked up at her, even more confused. "I've never heard anything about that. On the contrary, the Disteldorns were the ones who attacked the town, threatening to kill people."

Rosen got to her feet. "Does everybody in town believe that?" she asked, almost a whisper.

Gasto shrugged. "Of course, since it's what many of them saw. The castle was abandoned after that, and the town strove to forget the Disteldorns ever existed."

No, it wasn't that simple, she realized.

Kalt hadn't just tampered with Gasto's memory, but with everyone's in town, and even Varick's. And that meant no one knew the truth of what had happened that day long ago at the castle.

And no one knew who Kalt really was.

Rosen made for the door.

Gasto quickly got up and blocked her path. "You can't leave, Rosenrot. You must agree to marry me, first."

"You cannot force me!"

"Rosenrot, you don't understand. Kalt wants to execute you for thievery—"

Rosen dashed to the large window and thrust it open, hurrying out onto a small balcony beyond.

"I'm trying to save your life!" Gasto came, reaching for her.

She jumped before his hand could grab, falling into a patch of evergreen bushes below.

She hurried up, ignoring scratch marks, and bolted down the cobbled path into town.

Some of the autumn festivities were still going on as Rosen made her way past the town square, but the streets beyond were quieter.

An older man came out of the library when she passed and glanced her way: the library owner.

"Hello, Mr. Hans." She waved as she jogged past.

Light of the streetlamps reflected across his glasses and made his skin glint as if wet.

"Are you all right?" she suddenly wondered, slowing.

He looked so pale, his skin slick as porcelain.

He straightened his shoulders, and something cracked—a chip fell off of his chin.

A chip of porcelain.

Rosen started backwards, in wide-eyed horror, as the librarian moved towards her. No longer the man she once knew but a stiff, porcelain-skinned doll. Just like the strange servant she'd seen with Lord Kalt.

Another creaking announced a porcelain woman, a woman who Rosen once knew as a prolific baker.

Both came at her, and she raced to get away, footfalls pounding the street.

More creaking, and more porcelain figures appeared from side streets and alleys, calling her name, beckoning her with hands that promised to rip her apart.

"Rosenrot...Rosenrot..."

They surrounded her on all sides. She halted as more appeared on the street up ahead. She looked to the nearest door—the church—and hurried for it, praying it was unlocked.

The door gave way to her, and she shut it behind her, searching for a lock but there was none. She pushed what chairs were nearby against the door handle as it began to shake, then rushed down the church's center aisle.

Stained-glass windows shattered on either side as she ran; she covered her ears with elbow and hand. Porcelain heads and limbs reached over the windowsills, climbing like unsteady puppets into the church.

Rosen ran for the back, past a giant cross and rusty organ, to a back staircase, its steps spiraling upward. She could hear the golem creatures in pursuit, clacking feet echoing across the marble floor.

The spiral staircase led up onto the tower's belfry, a space open to the cool air and one large dangling bell. She bit back a shiver and looked down. The church's roofs were steep, and tendrils of fog made surfaces slick.

Golems continued up the stairs, calling her name through a ghostly moan.

There was no way out.

Rosen climbed onto the railing, clinging there, sweating, and debating the drop to the roof below.

"Varick!" she tried calling out, knowing it would be in vain.

The first golem's head peeked into the belfry.

"Please, God, let me live; or take my soul into Your arms," Rosen whispered.

And then, she let go.

The steep roof rushed to meet her.

She braced herself, suddenly realizing that her aim was off and she was falling too far to the left to catch the roof.

She held her single hand out, hoping there would be something to grab onto and slow the fall.

There wasn't.

She plummeted, seeing nothing but her doom towards the ground.

And then…arms scooped her up and lifted her through the air.

Rosen flailed, certain it was another monster, before seeing the ruby rose and Varick's silver eyes in the twilight. She stilled. "Varick, you found me?"

"And just in time, it seems. What did you do to make the townspeople so mad?" he said.

"I didn't! They're golems." She paused when he smirked.

"I'm trying to be funny. Is it working?"

"No," she replied tartly. "But thanks for catching me."

Varick landed on the edge of the church roof and leaped off: landing onto the roof of a shop, and leaping across onto the next.

Golems tried to follow from down below in the streets, their uneven gait unable to keep up.

"For future reference, jumping off of church towers isn't going to make you grow wings," he said.

She gave him a look that made him swallow his humor.

"I was heading to Pasto's, when I heard your cry," he told her.

"You heard my voice, above everything else?" She glanced back, taking in the aerial view of the town.

"I'll always hear your voice," he said, almost a whisper in her ear.

He landed on the dirt path at the edge of town, the one that led up into the forest and western foothills.

She planted a light kiss on his cheek before she could think, then blushed bright red, berating herself in her mind.

But Varick was almost smiling, even when his expression winced in pain from something.

"Are you hurt?" she asked.

The ruby rose around his neck didn't shine as much as it used to. In fact, most of the petals had gone strangely dark. Why was that?

"It's nothing." He carried her up the path, barely making a sound, as if his footsteps glided over the leaves too quickly.

"There's something I have to tell you. It's urgent. But I'm not sure if you'll believe me," she said, arm around his neck.

He glanced down at her. "I know you're not one to lie. I won't doubt you."

She sucked in a breath. "Remember that *Memory Shift* spell I found in Kalt's secret room? I know now what he's been using it for. Varick, the entire town believes it was the Disteldorns who attacked them. But you believe it was *them* who attacked and killed your family."

Varick's features frowned.

"Kalt has altered everyone's memories of that day—including yours."

Varick squinted, his eyebrows drawn down. "But..."

She turned her head away, watching the passing trees and

night fog. "I knew some of those people, Varick. They're dead—Kalt must have killed them and replaced them with those elaborate golems… And now he's trying to kill me, too."

Varick's gaze lowered to her.

"I won't let that happen," he stated firmly. "Do you think everyone in town is a golem by now?"

"No. Those still celebrating the festival ignored me," she guessed.

They reached the castle gate and its blood red vines. "How is it that your memory wasn't affected by the spell?" he asked. "Shouldn't you be like the other humans, and fear the Disteldorns?"

Rosen wondered. "I wasn't born in Freudendorf. I must have moved here long after the spell was first cast. The later renewing spells would have nothing to renew in me… Varick, the book said that the spell had to be renewed monthly. Kalt must have had the page open because that time is drawing near. If we can stop him before he renews it again…"

"We'll get our memories back," he finished. "But how do we find where Kalt will cast the spell? It could be anywhere."

He crossed the front courtyard and carried her indoors.

Rosen thought over the book's illustrations: star shapes that needed to be drawn in a circle around the intended target—in this case, the entire town and castle. The scope of the valley and foothills. There was only one way to manage something like that.

"The mountaintops," she surmised, sliding to her feet. "They're the only thing that surrounds us all."

She massaged her forehead. His arm around her shoulders kept her steady.

"I'll have Mrs. Moos make you something to clear

whatever it was that Pasto gave you," he said, the hint of a protective growl in his undertone.

"You should eat something, Varick. You look pale—well, more than usual."

Licht appeared, taking their cloaks, his foggy appearance somber.

"I've searched everywhere for Schatten, Master, but there's no sign of him. He did leave this note behind, though," he said meekly, and flinched as if expecting Varick's temper to erupt.

"...I see," was all Varick said, taking the note.

Rosen pressed against his shoulder to see and read it with him:

My clan has served your family long, but it was never something that I wanted. I was simply born into the fate, and did as I was told, putting up with you.

But my family died trying to protect you Disteldorns, and I can never forgive you for that. I've found a new residence to call my own, now, and so I leave your service.

—Schatten

Varick tossed the paper to the floor; it drifted slowly down.

He took Rosen's hand and led her into the kitchens without a word.

Rosen tried to calm her stomach by eating the potato soup Mrs. Moos handed her, but the memory of people turning into golems wouldn't leave her mind.

Varick kept pressing his hand to his chest, as if fighting a phantom pain. She watched as he kept trying to shrug it off.

"I thought you had run off, at first. I'm sorry I doubted you," he admitted to her, staring down at the hot soup mug in his hands.

A smile tugged at her lips. "Jealous a little?" she said with a smirk.

He chuckled. "A little."

A sound rumbled beyond the kitchen window, though she didn't remember seeing any heavy clouds.

"Dearie me, I hope the storm winds don't ruin all your hard work in the gardens," commented Mrs. Moos, stirring a hot cauldron.

Rosen almost laughed. That was the least of their worries, right now.

"Master! *Master!*" Licht came running in, with a creaking, wheezing Sterbetod following.

"What?" Varick snapped, a hint of pain lining his tone.

"You—you won't believe this, but it seems the entire town is marching up to the gate. Armed and carrying torches," said Licht. "Master, they're storming the castle!"

"WHAT?" VARICK EXCLAIMED, RISING QUICKLY. The sound wasn't thunder from clouds but from a crowd of angry voices. "Why are they doing this? And why *now*?" he growled.

They hurried after Varick, up to the balcony which overlooked the front of the castle and the gate beyond. Rosen spied hundreds of lights from torches. Chants and cries echoed the air, and she spied Gasto at the head.

"The Beast of the Night must die!"

"It's time we avenge those the Disteldorn beasts murdered!"

"This castle has scared us away from the mountains long enough. Now we will make the beast scared of *us*!"

The gate rattled as the crowd pushed against the rods and tried climbing over.

Varick's mouth hung slack. "They really believe my family were the ones who attacked *them*?" He shook his head, incredulous.

Rosen cupped her hand over his. "It's time we found out the truth." She nodded her chin up to the night sky, to the surrounding tops of the mountains. On the side of the peak to their right, a fire burned—a light in the dark for someone who was up there despite the chill of autumn night.

It could only be one person.

Varick clutched his chest and nodded. "Time is running out. Let's end this." He gave her hand an affectionate squeeze.

She wanted to ask what he meant by time running out—it felt like he meant something more than the spell—but Licht brought them their cloaks and Varick lifted her in his arms. Before she could protest being carried, he leaped off the balcony onto a lower roof, running along the edge and vaulting to the next. She held on for dear life.

The Disteldorn servants waved, and she prayed they would stay safe somehow. The townspeople's shouts followed after them.

Varick cleared the castle and landed in an oak in the gardens, from there leaping across the hedges and into the forest, up the mountainside.

Varick climbed the distance with ease. The campfire grew brighter by the second, up on a flattened stretch near the rocky peak. A coating of snow covered everything there.

He set her down at the forest's edge, before the wide empty stretch of rock.

The fire was big enough to light the whole area, and it showed Kalt's stooped figure: drawing one final line through the snow and soil with a cane—a line that completed the star symbol she'd seen in the spell book.

"Let me handle things. I can't have you getting hurt," said Varick.

She made a face. "As if. I'm destroying that symbol."

He flashed her a smile that made her heart flutter. "Fine. But let me handle Kalt." He brushed a finger down her cheek. Only two petals left on the ruby rose glowed. "Stay safe."

Varick started out onto the barren, snow-covered stretch, head held high and regal.

Kalt spotted his approach and straightened. "So, you've figured it out, have you?"

He regarded Varick coldly, then snapped his fingers.

From all around the clearing, golems rose—clay and inhuman, their gaping mouths jagged with rows of fangs, heaving up from the rock.

"I suppose it was only a matter of time."

"Give us our memories back, Lord Kalt, and perhaps I can overlook this," said Varick.

Kalt gave a grim laugh. "Oh, I highly doubt you'd be able to. But then, what does it matter now? That girl has ruined everything. You're close to death, and that means my careful plan will collapse."

"What are you going on about?" Varick demanded.

"I must restart things—give you a fresh, new memory. Take the girl out of your life."

Anger raged across Varick's features. But before he could do anything, Kalt clicked his tongue and pointed, "Seize him!"

The golems rushed in as one, lumbering in their uneven gait.

Varick leaped; he punched his fist through the first golem's head, shattering clay and dust.

He turned in the air, kicking his foot up into another golem's chin, breaking the head off.

Both creatures tumbled to the ground. But more and more came, and again Varick leaped, smashing through more golems.

One caught his cape and threw him against the ground, where it pummeled its heavy fists into Varick's chest.

Varick rolled out of the way, coughing, and with a burst of vempar speed wove through the crowd of golems, smashing his right fist through them. But they pressed in all around him like walls, and his energy couldn't last forever.

Something slapped across Varick's cheek.

He roundhouse kicked another golem before turning to see what it was.

"I've been wanting to do that for sooo long," said Schatten, hovering in the air at his height.

Varick snarled and slashed his hand out to grab the shadow nymiad, but Schatten slipped to the side easily. "Is *this* who you're serving now? This warlock?"

Schatten's purple frown glowed. "I don't serve anyone anymore. I'm simply earning myself land, where I can build a place for other nymiads and rule, no longer having to deal with you vempars and humans." The shadows cast by the firelight and moon writhed around Schatten and shot forward.

Varick vaulted into the air, back-flipping behind a golem which he then kicked forward for Schatten's shadows to catch. "Fine, so you hate me. But why would you hurt Rosenrot?" his voice raised.

"I wanted your heart to break. Just as mine did when my family was murdered while defending yours!" Schatten's lip and fists trembled with rage, and he threw the golem aside, sending more shadows forward.

"You could have left. I wasn't making you stay," Varick said as he landed on top of a golem, tricking the shadows again.

"And leave the castle, the only tie to my family I had left? Oh, no no." Schatten shook his head, fingers directing ribbons of shadow climbing up the golem.

Varick jumped away onto a second golem.

"I'm not going anywhere. It's *you* I want gone, so that the castle can be made mine."

A shadow caught Varick's leg and dragged him down to the ground. He spat out a mouthful of snow, blood mixed in.

"But if Kalt wants you alive, I guess I could put up with you being *my* servant, for a change. I'm sure Kalt can make your mind more submissive."

Golem fists pounded down on him as shadows held Varick to the snow.

"Don't worry. The spell is almost ready, and then your pitiful love and pain will come to an end."

Varick struggled to rise, but golems piled over and around him. He didn't have much strength left; he could feel his life bleeding out with the fading ruby rose…

Rosen watched from the forest edge as the fight first began, then crept her way around the clearing while the golems focused on Varick.

She hurried, crouching, coming towards the hot fire and the nearby symbol from the other side.

She noticed the spell book, not far from Kalt's foot. His gaze was on Varick as she crawled forward, the tall bonfire between them.

She inched closer to the star symbol drawn in the snow, reached out her hand to the nearest point, and rubbed the lines away, trying to do it quietly.

Something crushed down on her wrist and she yelped in pain.

Kalt looked down at her, suddenly there, his boot pinning her arm. "Well, well, what should we do about *you*?" Kalt pretended to wonder. His hand gripped her from the back of the neck and lifted her up, her feet dangling. "I don't think I could get much use out of a deformed creature like yourself. Except maybe to turn your corpse into another porcelain golem to serve me," he mused.

Rosen kicked her feet and screamed, clawing her fingernails down his arm. But he only laughed. With the cane in his other hand, he began to redraw the star's point.

Varick heard Rosenrot's scream. Rage pulsed through his body, adrenaline filling his muscles. With a final burst of strength, he shoved up, forcing golems tumbling off him and breaking the binds of the shadows.

His fist met Schatten's chest before the nymiad could back away, and his shadowy form skidded and rolled across the snowy expanse, clear to the other side.

Varick grabbed one golem by the leg, hoisting and swinging it in the air, plowing it through the other golems that were left, like a blade cutting down grass. He headed towards Kalt, flinging the golem his way. "Let her go, I'm warning you," he growled. Pain lanced through his chest with every breath, but he kept his mind focused on her—only her.

Kalt moved in one swift motion, striking his cane across Rosenrot's head and tossing her unconscious body behind him.

Varick's breath hitched as she lay there. He roared and charged across the snow at Kalt.

Kalt swirled his fingers and cane about, and the silver crescent moons on his robes began to glow and pull free of the fabric: They hovered in the air, gaining solidity and growing. He jabbed the cane forward, and the moons solid as blades spun through the air towards Varick.

Varick raised his arm to block one, and the blade almost

took off his wrist. He held his hand in place, letting it heal, and tried to dodge the other five blades coming at him.

He ducked under and swerved, but as they passed, the spinning crescents turned back around midair; they were fast. He fell sideways, narrowly avoiding a fatal slice across the throat.

Kalt sent forth more crescent blades, the bonfire's light glinting off his grin.

Varick knew he saw his weakness: the slowing of his movements, the pain, trouble breathing. The time for the spell was drawing nearer. He flicked his wrist, testing if it had healed.

"Why are you doing this, Kalt? What is it you want? What can you get from Freudendorf and me that you couldn't just get somewhere else?" he demanded, panting.

A volley of moon blades came at his legs and chest. He vaulted high into the air to avoid them, but a blade separate from the rest appeared suddenly—digging into his right breast while he fell to the ground.

The force of the blade slammed him onto his back, pinning him to the snow and rock, forcing the air out of his lungs, a new pain lancing through his chest.

A second crescent moon pierced through his right side, pinning him more firmly to the ground.

"So many *why's* and *what's*," mused Kalt. "But since you'll be forgetting everything soon, I suppose I could give you an answer." He took out from his robes a satin pouch, untied it and sprinkled a handful of glittering orange substance across the drawn star symbol.

A hum of energy filled the air, raising the hair along the nape of Varick's neck.

"I've always despised the Altered and mages, the things they can do that no human can—at least, not without the proper ingredients," said Kalt. "I cannot touch the coding of the world as the mages once did, but with the aid of a special salt, I can still do *things*." He jiggled the pouch. "A rare salt, which happens to form alongside the regular salt in these mines, here. Not many know of its special properties other than for flavor. I came across it during my travels, not far from this valley. That is what brought me to Freudendorf.

"This town had been built and ruled by the Disteldorn vempar family for many years: created to be a haven for the Altered, a place hidden away from human hunters and prejudice. I could hardly believe my luck finding it; it was like discovering buried treasure! And with my powers and golems, it was easy to take the Disteldorns by surprise and kill them off."

Varick stared; he wasn't sure if he was shaking from the overwhelming shock or from rage. Kalt's grin flashed sharp as a knife.

"I decided to keep you alive though, Varick, as part of the spell I cast over the town. That cursed mage artifact I'd been carrying with me finally served a purpose: keeping you alive."

"What did you do to the town?" Varick gritted out.

Kalt gave a dry laugh. "You've already guessed it, haven't you? Freudendorf is a town of vempars, but my spell makes them believe they are human and see the Disteldorns as evil beasts.

"I made them fear you and the mountains near your castle so they would abandon the salt mines, fearing the Beast of the Night and its curse. And since then, I've been able to harvest the rare salt in secret; and harvest the blood of vempars, as well, making a profit by selling portions at the black market. Oh, I keep most of the salt for myself; and vempar blood mixed with this special ingredient keeps me young and lets me heal. Some vempars wake up from the spell, now and then, and I have to sadly end their lives and replace them with human-like golems. That's been the only downside; I don't like to diminish my blood harvest."

Varick fought to breathe, squeezing his eyes shut. "But…vempars need life-energy to survive."

"Yes, and I make sure that all of the town's food has some in it," replied Kalt.

"But…but…" Varick struggled to comprehend the truth, and slowly all the pieces of the puzzle fell into place. "You deceived me from the very beginning. The town was my family's to watch over, and I failed them. You never saved my life—you took it away. You took my family away from me!"

The star symbol in the snow started to glow an ember orange. The *Memory Shift* spell was beginning to renew.

Varick grabbed the sharp edges of the moon blades and tore them free of his body, then rose and slung them at Kalt.

The blades sunk into Kalt's abdomen. His sneering grin didn't falter as he pulled them out and the skin beneath healed. "I already told you, I can heal myself like a vempar, thanks to you."

Kalt motioned with his cane and the moon blades all re-gathered, coming at Varick in a volley. Too many to dodge, too fast.

Varick cast about for something, anything, when his hand found a golem leg.

He hoisted the golem and swung it as he would a mace—knocking moon blades aside, some sticking into the clay creature.

Rosen's head pounded as she opened her eyes.

Shapes shifted before her, slowly taking form: Varick and

Kalt battling.

She forced herself onto her hand and knees, and crawled forward, inch by agonizing inch, until she was in reach of the drawn star, its lines now glowing with power.

She swiped her hand across the snow and shallow dirt to ruin the line, and the star's energy burned her skin. She bit back a yelp.

Sucking in a breath through her nose, she prepared herself for the pain and swiped her entire arm across the lines forming a star point—wiping them out and burning her entire arm.

The star hissed, and its glow flickered.

Before Kalt could call the moon blades back around, Varick charged, slamming the golem's body into Kalt—the tips of the blades that were sticking out of the clay stabbing into Kalt.

Varick grabbed another blade, its edge cutting into his palm, and he grabbed Kalt by the collar. "Even vempars can die," he told him, and drove the blade through Kalt's chest, aiming for the heart.

Kalt screamed, an agonized howl. Blood dripped down his front as he fell backwards into the snow, dark robes billowing around him.

The star symbol sputtered and hissed until it finally winked out, and the *Memory Shift* spell was broken.

Memories flooded back to Varick, back to Licht and those in the castle, back to Gasto and the townspeople as they worked to break down the castle door and crawl in through windows. They ceased their rampage, and many slumped to the ground, heads held in their hands, tears falling, as they remembered who they really were and their kind rulers, the Disteldorns.

Rosen hugged her injured arm with the stump of her left and pushed up on her knees to stand. Varick's silver gaze met hers, and he took one step forward before suddenly clutching his chest and collapsing onto his back.

"Varick!" She dashed to his side, kneeling, touching his cheek with her blistered hand. "Where are you hurt? Why aren't you healing?"

He stared up at her, a small serene smile on his lips. His hand reached up, cupping her face. "This isn't something that can be healed," he said, voice faint and hoarse.

Rosen blinked through sudden tears. "I don't understand."

His lips parted. "I lied to Licht—to everyone—about this cursed necklace," he said.

"You mean, that if you fall in love, it'll make you ugly? Oh come on, Varick. I would never care how you looked," Rosen told him.

He shook his head, a slight, painful movement. "Not ugly. The curse is that I would die. I'm...I'm dying, Rosenrot. This necklace is all that's been keeping me alive—its power sustaining my body, ever since my heart was irreparably damaged."

Rosen looked down at him, his words slowly sinking in. Every time his hand had pressed to his chest, it was because the necklace was killing him. It was because of her.

"Varick...I didn't mean to...if I'd known... I'm so sorry." Tears tumbled down her cheeks. His thumb brushed them away.

"I'm not sorry," he said. "My life was cold...lonely...before you. If getting to love you means I have to die...then it was worth it."

The last of the glowing ruby rose petals on the necklace flickered out.

"I wasn't good at showing it, but...I love you, Rosenrot." His hand slid, fingers caressing down her cheek to her chin, and then his arm fell limp and the light faded from his silver eyes. Strands of black hair fell about his pale face.

"I love you, Varick." Rosen squeezed her hand over his, tears drowning out her vision. Pain greater than any kind tore at her heart while she sobbed, bending to press her forehead to his chest. Only the sudden crunching sound of boots made her look up. She took the necklace off of Varick and tossed it away; he would no longer be under its curse.

Gasto came trotting across the snow to her. When he saw Varick's body, he slowed to a stop. "No...oh no. What have we done? Lord Varick..." He came nearer, cheeks as tear stained as hers. "Wait, where is Kalt? Where is that twisted monster?"

Rosen straightened and looked about. The place where Kalt had fallen, supposedly dead, was empty.

"If he ever shows his face again…!" Gasto's fists shook.

He made his way around the bonfire and picked something up, bringing it near. "A spell book?" he muttered, turning it over.

Rosen bolted to her feet and snatched the book from him, startling the young man—or rather, vempar. Now the long canines which all of Freudendorf's people had made sense. She set the book on the ground and flipped through the aged pages.

There had to be something.

Surely, there had to be…

Her fingers slid over page after page. She chewed her lip, until the drawing of a heart caught her eye: It was illustrated in detail below the title *Organ Remake*.

The spell could create a heart, but it required someone else's heart to take form: dividing a single heart into two, and thereby shortening the lifespan of the other person.

Rosen smoothed the page to keep it open as she hurried over to the star symbol, knelt and scooped up what sparkling orange salt she could see from the lines.

Gasto watched with a baffled expression as she carried the special salt over to Varick and sat before the spell book.

She poured the salt into a careful pile on Varick's chest, over where his heart should be, and drew a sun-like symbol the book showed. Then she took some of the salt in her burnt hand and pressed it to her chest.

The book stated that an artifact able to connect with the natural-energy of their surroundings was needed for non-mages in order to activate the spell. But the cane, and anything else Kalt had had with him, was missing.

Rosen had nothing to use but her hope.

She closed her eyes and with her mind tried to feel for the life that made up the world around her, but it was beyond her grasp. "Please...please let this work," she prayed, trying again.

Something plopped into her lap. She looked to see the necklace—a mage artifact, Kalt had called it. Her stump of an arm pressed it close to herself, and again she focused, this time feeling a warm glow flowing towards her, weaving around the salt pressed to her heart and connecting with the salt on Varick.

Her chest felt hotter and hotter; a pink glow in the shape of a beating heart exited through her skin. She watched the ghost-like image float across the path of energy and down into Varick's chest. The light of the glow faded as it passed through his skin.

His chest pulsed with a faint light for several seconds, then the light winked out and the energy of the spell vanished.

Rosen let down her hand.

"Did it work?" Gasto peered at him.

She lowered to Varick's face, pressing her fingers to the side of his neck.

There was nothing...no, a deep pulse was slowly starting to form, taking rhythm. She watched expectantly as Varick's eyelids began to flicker, and then his eyes flickered open, gazing into hers.

Gasto nearly fell over in shock.

Varick seemed at first confused, as if he'd been somewhere else, but then he lifted his hand to stroke her cheek. "How did you...?" he began, but she bent down, pressing her lips against his.

He wrapped his arms around her, embracing, holding her close.

16

LORD VARICK REOPENED THE SALT mines, and Freudendorf once again made trade deals with neighboring villages and towns. Wealth returned to the valley, and the people were finally able to set about making repairs and improvements. Of course, the town's true nature remained a guarded secret, a haven for those in need…

Rosen finished dusting the last bookcase shelf in the little town library. The place would need a lot of care and love now that its owner was gone.

"Don't worry. I'll look after it," came a voice.

She spun around to see Gasto entering, his shirtsleeves rolled up and dirt-smudged.

"It's just one more thing to add to the never-ending list of things to be done around here," he said.

She was glad to see him, which was a strange feeling considering the past. "And we appreciate your help," she replied. Ever since he regained his memory, he'd donated all his time and effort into helping repair the town.

"So, you and Varick are tying the knot, hm? A happy, romantic couple?" said Gasto, and he gave her a pointed look.

Rosen felt her cheeks blush. "It just…sort of happened. I don't know. We have a lot more in common than I first thought. And he's really changed. He's quite sweet…" She started playing with the braid in her hair.

Gasto broke out in a lopsided grin. "I'm teasing. Practically the whole town knew it was going to happen. Honestly, I'm surprised you waited this long."

Rosen ducked her head and stifled a smile.

"I won't pretend I'm not jealous. Finding real love would be nice," he said. "Maybe I'll wait for it, as you did."

She patted his shoulder. "There's a girl out there just perfect for you. You'll bump into each other, one day. You'll see."

His lips drew a sideways smile.

"Have you heard any news of your parents' whereabouts?" she asked.

Gasto's parents—he'd remembered after the Kalt incident—had been taken away during human riots in a neighboring country, and their servants had disguised Gasto and brought him here to hide with his family's old friends: the Disteldorns.

"I have. Word says they were last seen in a village in France, several years back. One of my servants just left to go investigate." His hand fisted. "If they're being held captive somewhere, I'll find them."

"You have our full support," she assured.

She put away the dustrags and followed Gasto out the door into daylight.

Rosen turned in place, surveying the fresh paint, new wood, and flower planters of all the buildings around the town square. Everything was finally starting to look nice and repaired after months of work. It was satisfying to see. And a sweet scent hung in the spring air from flowering trees.

"My lady?" Varick was waiting by the black carriage, dressed in a fine blue suit with ruffle cuffs and cravat. He offered her his arm. She took it, using her stump arm.

"We'll see you tomorrow, Lord Disteldorn, Lady soon-to-be Disteldorn! The new fountain should be finished by then." Gasto flourished a bow.

Varick helped her into the carriage, and the black stallion unicorn pulled them along, following the road to the uphill path.

Rosen watched out the window as their castle rose into view ahead. Workers were busy about the stonework and doors, replacing rotted wood and clearing off mold from outer walls. Already the place looked much brighter, even if it kept its gothic design.

Varick hurried to check on the gardens as soon as they pulled up to the garage. She laughed, following after him. Ever since he'd planted pumpkin seeds, he'd been worrying over his pumpkin patch in the garden. Now he bent low, inspecting the tiny beginnings of leaf tendrils. "Do they need more water? More sunlight? No…ah, I don't know! I'm better at growing mushrooms than pumpkins." He scratched at his head.

Fee-ee! The red thistle pixit flittered past them, giggling.

"It'll be fine." Rosen chuckled, patting his back. "Just show a little patience."

She walked over to where rose vines were starting to bloom, covering an arched trellis tunnel. Sunlight dappled the path between the trellis bars, and the mix of red and purple roses smelled as sweet as perfume.

"At least these seem to be doing well," said Varick, coming alongside her in the tunnel, taking in the view.

His fingers entwined with hers and he pressed a kiss to her cheek. "You've brought so much life to this place, and to me," he said. "I should berate you for shortening your lifespan for my sake, but…I'm so happy, being able to be with you again."

Rosen smiled and nudged him with her head. "It's worth it. Besides, we share the same lifespan now, so even if it is shorter, at least we'll stay together. Which reminds me, I hope the church's repairs hurry up. Our official wedding day is in two weeks!"

Varick laughed. "What was it you just told me: have patience?"

She shoved his shoulder playfully.

Someone coughed, and they both turned and looked down.

There stood Schatten at the edge of the trellis tunnel, his shadowy suit faded under the bright noon sun. He shuffled forward just a bit, moving into the shade. "I heard of your generous offer and came to…discuss it," he said, not meeting their gazes.

Varick stepped forward. "Schatten, I haven't forgotten what you said, or how you felt. I was an unkind master to you, and for that I am sorry. Just because your family served me doesn't mean you should have to as well. This valley is meant to be a haven for vempars, for Altered, and that includes nymiads too." He pulled out a document and handed it down to Schatten. "The southern foothills of the valley are now for the nymiads. I trust you can oversee matters there, and make a suitable home for your kind?"

Schatten took the document slowly, a tremor in his hands. "You're…you're really doing this for us?"

Varick inclined his head.

Schatten's purple eyes moistened. "Thank you. Thank you." He turned so that they couldn't see his sleeve wipe his face. "Nymiads will finally have a safe place they can belong." He hugged the paper to his chest, turned around and bowed quickly before he hurried to leave.

"Ah, Schatten," Varick called out, and the nymiad paused, looking back. "You'd better be at our wedding—it's my last order, as your former master. It wouldn't be the same without all of those who helped raise me."

Schatten's purple smile flashed. "I suppose, if you insist."

Licht peeked around a corner as Schatten left. "It was awfully kind of you to forgive his betrayal, Master," he said.

Varick patted his foggy shoulder with affection. "His parents and sister died fighting Kalt to protect me. This was the least I could do. And besides, we're all family in the end." He wrapped his other arm around Rosenrot. "And I cannot wait to add one more to it, in two weeks."

Rosen grinned, glancing down at the ring on her finger: a diamond in the shape of a rose.

Thank you for reading! The setting for this book is a fictional town in the Austrian Alps. When I was little, my family took many road trips to Salzburg, Austria: a charming city with a grand view of the sharp, dramatic mountains. This is also where The Sound of Music movie was filmed!

Another cool thing about Salzburg are the salt mines. It was a fascinating experience for me going down into the deep mountain tunnels and seeing where the miners used to work. We got to ride on a boat across a still, quiet underground lake and then ride down a slide which miners used to use to reach lower levels more quickly.

There was so much to see and do in Salzburg, that the beautiful city quickly captured my heart, and I knew that one day I would love to write a story that was inspired by this area.

If you read Beast of the Night and want to share it with other readers, please consider leaving a review on Amazon and Goodreads. This makes a huge difference for indie authors like me! Reviews help boost a book on retailer websites so that it'll be found by more readers, which in turn helps support the author.

You can be the first to learn about new releases, get bonus content, free ebooks and book sales by signing up for my newsletter at:

eerawls.com

Above all, thanks be to God, who makes me able. To learn more about Him, visit:
PeaceWithGod.net/where-is-god

Reader Insider Vault

Here You'll Get Access To:

- My Curated **No-Spice Book Lists**
- Bookish **News**, *Recs & Merch*
- **Behind the Scenes** details + First Looks + *Fun Bonuses* of my books
- **Free ebooks** & more!
- My **Exclusive Newsletter** & Substack: *where you can follow my author updates & fun random finds!*

eerawls.com

Scan QR Code:

THE ALTEREDVERSE

Books in the *Alteredverse* are standalone tales that take place in our world, at different points in time, and they often feature the humanoid Altered Ones (read **Portal to Eartha** for the origin story of the Altered).

They can be read in any order. Some books take place during our time, and some far into the future. To see the full Timeline of events, and where each book fits, visit:

eerawls.com/alteredverse

If you enjoyed the world of *Beast of the Night*, be sure to check out the other books in the *Alteredverse*. Also, check out the series **Draev Guardians** that takes place in the *Earthaverse* — the twin planet to our world (it can be read at any time and separately from *Alteredverse* books).

Suggested reading order:

- *Frost, Winter's Lonely Guardian*
- *Portal to Eartha*
- *Beast of the Night*
- *Madness Solver in Wonderland*

Frost, Winter Guardian and current resident of Boston. For centuries he's watched over the winter seasons, and now he longs to end his work and move on from this world. But for that, he needs a replacement…and the human girl and artist, Norah, might be the one.

A Jack Frost reimagining full of heart and wintery chill!

Portal to Eartha:

Future Japan.
A clue to a secret portal world.
The only hope for Lotus, an Altered girl with the gift of
Healing, on the run from the mafia.
You can get the ebook version FREE by joining
my newsletter!

Strayborn
Elemental Manipulation is a tricky business as Cyrus, a girl who can manipulate metal, and Aken the last Scourgeblood, are about to find out, in a world that is determined to either use them or destroy them…

See all purchase links at eerawls.com

How You Can Help

Reviews help boost a book on retailer websites so that it'll be found by more readers, which in turn helps support the author. *If you read Beast of the Night and want to share it with others, please consider leaving a review on Amazon and Goodreads—this makes a huge difference for indie authors like me!*

8 Ways to Support an Indie Author:

See a list of all the ways you can help support my work, as well as other indie authors!
Scan the QR code:

AUTHOR

E.E. Rawls is the product of a traveling family, who even lived in Italy for 6 years. She loves exploring the unknown, whether it be in a forest, the ruins of a forgotten castle, or in the pages of a book. Her brain runs on coffee, cuddly cats, and the mysterious beauty of nature while she writes.

Visit her online at **eerawls.com** and get free access to the Reader Insider Vault: